# PATRICIA
# ST JOHN

## The Tanglewoods' Secret

British Library Cataloguing-in-Publication Data.
A catalogue record of this book is available from the British Library.

Printed and bound in India by Thomson Press

Cover design by Go Ballistic
Internal design and layout by Author and Publisher Services

Scripture Union is an international Christian charity working with churches in
more than 130 countries.

Thank you for purchasing this book. Any profits from this book support SU in
England and Wales to bring the good news of Jesus Christ to children, young
people and families and to enable them to meet God through the Bible and prayer.

Find out more about our work and how you can get involved at:
www.scriptureunion.org.uk (England and Wales)
www.suscotland.org.uk (Scotland)
www.suni.co.uk (Northern Ireland)
www.scriptureunion.org (USA)
www.su.org.au (Australia)

# Contents

# 1

# Holiday plans

It was a beautiful home where Philip and I lived with Aunt Margaret – a white house on the slope of the hill behind which the sun set, with a garden and an orchard where cowslips and clovers ran riot under the apple trees. Philip and I slept in the two top attics, with the doors open so that we could shout across. I could never quite make up my mind which window I loved best, Philip's or mine. Philip's gave me a feeling of security, for it looked out on the garden, hedged in with pines and the shelter of the near green hills with their bracken and gorse rising beyond. But mine gave me a thrill of adventure, for it looked out on the great Worcestershire plain with its fields and its cherry blossom, and its far, far hills, somewhere away in Herefordshire, where I had never been.

I loved those hills. Sometimes they looked so green and close by, sometimes so misty and far away. I looked on them as a sort of fairyland where I might go some day when I was grown up. And when Philip came in to sit on my bed in the morning to listen to the first bird songs, or to watch the flaming sunrise over the plain, we used to tell each other stories about them, and about the strange beasts that lived upon their slopes.

Philip was nearly 11, a year and a half older than I, and I loved him more than anyone else on earth. He was a gentle, thoughtful boy, slow in coming to conclusions, but completely dogged in carrying them out. Ever since I could remember he had been my friend, my protector and my comforter. And, except at day school, we had never been apart. We were about as different as a brother and sister could be. Philip was well built, with serious blue eyes and a round, placid face. I was small and thin, with dark, untidy hair and a sharp chin. Philip was good and obedient. I was wild and did what I liked. Aunt Margaret openly loved Philip, but she shook her head over me and said that I took years off her life.

At the time of my story we had been five years with Aunt Margaret, and had forgotten what Mother and Father looked like. I was 4 years old when they had sailed for India. Of course, Mother had meant to come home long ago, but the war had stopped her. I don't think I really wanted her to come back. Aunt Margaret was so fond of telling me what a disappointment I should be to my poor mother, that I hoped to put off the discovery as long as possible. In her letters, she always sounded as though she loved me very much. But that, I supposed, was because she did not know me. In any case, when she came she would like Philip much better than me, because grown-ups always did. And Philip would like her, because Philip liked everybody, and I would much rather have Philip all to myself. So I pushed away the thought of Mother's homecoming, and thought about it as little as possible.

This story begins on the first day of our Easter holidays, when Philip came into my room in his pyjamas at half-past six in the morning. He curled up on the end of my bed with his notebook and pencil in his hand. Together we leaned our elbows on the windowsill to watch birds and to make plans.

Birdwatching was our great hobby that holiday. We had a notebook in which we recorded each different kind of bird we saw, and everything we noticed about it – its song, its nest, its habits. Philip had made the book himself, and it was beautifully neat and accurate. He did all the writing and I painted the eggs when we found them. But my drawings were not particularly lifelike.

Philip longed for a camera with which to photograph his nests. "If only I could take photographs of them," he would say, over and over again, "I might be a great naturalist. My book might even be printed."

But the cheapest camera in the shop windows cost pounds, and our money box held a fraction of what we needed even though we had been saving for weeks and weeks. We emptied the coins on to the quilt, and counted them over again, just in case we'd made a mistake the time before. But we hadn't. Philip sighed deeply.

"At this rate, I shall be going to boarding school by the time I get that camera," he said. "I wish we could earn some money, Ruth."

We gazed out into the garden rather sadly, racking our brains for some plan. But nothing brilliant suggested itself to us. Below us, April had touched the fruit trees, and blossom foamed like a soft white sea over the plain. Our own damson trees were white and lacy, and I could see nests of primroses around their roots and golden daffodil trumpets shining in the sun. I looked across to the hills, but they were hidden in the early haze of a spring morning. All of a sudden Philip half dived out of the window in his eagerness.

"Tree creeper!" he hissed. "On the plum!"

I leaned out beside him and we watched together – a neat brown bird running up the tree, tapping the bark for insects. Philip was all alert now, noting every slightest pose and gesture. He hardly drew breath until the little creature had spread its wings and disappeared round the corner. Then out came pen and notebook, and my brother was absorbed for five minutes.

"Ruth," he said eagerly, looking up at the end of that time, "we must get to the woods early today and have plenty of time. And Ruth, I was thinking in bed last night, we ought to have a naturalist's headquarters. We ought to build a place where we could keep pencils and rough paper and provisions in tins, instead of always carrying them with us, because we shall go every day all the holidays. And we must escape early before Aunt Margaret thinks of things we ought to do."

"We'll race through our holiday jobs," I announced, "and I'll be as good as gold, so she'll hardly notice me, and she won't watch me. When I've swept and dusted in the drawing room, I'll just slip out before she thinks of anything else. And if she asks where we've been, we'll say we've been getting wood, and we'll bring a little back with us to make it true. But I don't see why we should have to work at all in our holidays! I know what I'll do. I'll dress quick, and go down now and help Aunt Margaret with breakfast to make her think how good I'm being!"

In ten minutes' time, I duly presented myself in the scullery, arrayed in a clean pinny, with my hair in perfect order.

"Can I help you, Aunt Margaret?" I asked meekly. "I got up early in case you might need me."

As I was noted for my lateness in the mornings, my aunt looked rather astonished.

"Thank you, Ruth," she answered pleasantly, hiding her amazement, "you can lay the table for me. I should be very glad."

Everything went smoothly. Philip and I bolted our breakfast and sat bottling up our impatience while Uncle Peter and Aunt Margaret sipped their second cups of coffee, discussing the day ahead. Then Uncle Peter went off, and Aunt Margaret turned to us.

"And what plans have you two made?" she asked. Philip had the answer all ready. "As soon as we've done our holiday jobs, we're going to get wood in the Cowleighs, Aunt Margaret," he replied, in his sweetest voice.

"Very well," answered my aunt a little doubtfully, "but you must remember I need your help in the mornings. Ruth is old enough to assist in the house now. She shall start with wiping up and doing the drawing room, and then we'll see."

I could be quick when I liked, and I wiped up the breakfast things in an astonishingly short time. Then, without any further consultation with my aunt, I seized the broom and duster and made for the drawing room. I poked the dust wildly round the linoleum with the broom, and flicked it off the ledges at top speed. I could not see the dustpan, but wasted no time about it. I gathered up my little heap and shoved it under the carpet. Then I tiptoed back to the kitchen, replaced the broom and duster, and was out of the front door like a streak of lightning.

Out and free on an April morning, with the sun shining, and the birds singing, and the lambs bleating! I tore round the back like a whirlwind and pounced upon

Philip all unexpectedly, nearly knocking him over. But he was quite used to me by now, and was not much alarmed.

"Finished already?" he said, rather surprised.

"Yes. Haven't you?"

"No," he answered. "I've got to chop these sticks into little bundles for kindling wood. It will take ages."

"Oh," I cried, "we can't wait! You've made quite enough of those silly bundles. No one will know you haven't chopped them all up if they can't see the rest. Quick – give those sticks to me!"

And before my dutiful brother could protest, I had heaved the remainder into the ditch and was kicking the dead leaves over them.

"And think," I shouted, prancing up and down, "how quickly we shall find them when we are sent to get more!" And, with a final leap, I was away across the orchard; away through the clean wet grass all starred with primroses and flecked with blossom petals, and out through the gap in the back hedge like a young rabbit, with Philip at my heels.

The gap in the hedge was our own special right of way, and no one else knew about it. Aunt Margaret could see the gate from the kitchen window, and sometimes we preferred to keep our comings and goings to ourselves. So we had found a gap, behind the hen house, invisible to anyone else on account of the overhanging branches which we brushed aside. It led out into another meadow which led to the road, which in turn led to our woods.

Once in the road I danced and shouted like a crazy young thing. It was sheer joy to be alive on such a morning. Philip followed more soberly, his eyes glued to the hedges, now and then stopping to listen or to watch. I did not wait for him. I felt as though spring had got into my feet. I think I scared away most of the birds before Philip came anywhere near them.

I vaulted the gate that led through the meadow, and stood still for a minute watching the staid mother sheep with their merry long-legged lambs, leaping, like me, among the daisies. And as I watched, one of the lambs with a smudged nose and black stockings suddenly saw me and came rushing towards me, uttering little bleats of welcome. I squatted down and held out my arms. He ran straight into them, and started licking my face with his eager warm tongue.

"Philip!" I cried. "Philip, look what's happening!"

Philip was beside me by this time, and together we knelt in the grass while the lamb prodded us, licked us, and leaped from one lap to another. As we played, an old shepherd came and leaned over the gate, smiling at us.

"That's the little orphan," he explained. "He's bottle-fed, and he's not afraid of anyone. The other sheep push him away, so off he goes on his own. He's always up to mischief, the little rascal!"

The lamb at this moment leaped from my knee and ran to the gate. The old man stooped and picked it up.

"He knows my voice all right, don't he?" he remarked, smilingly. Then, tucking it inside his coat, he turned away towards the farm.

"That's a new shepherd," I said to Philip. "I've never seen him before."

"I have," answered Philip. "He's over from Cradley for the lambing season. I think he's called Mr Tandy. Come on, Ruth! We're wasting time."

He jumped up, and we raced across the open meadow with the wind blowing my plaits out behind me. Then over a stile, and we were standing in our woods.

# 2

# The wigwam

Philip and I left the path and fought our way through the young trees which seemed all bound together with honeysuckle tendrils. At last we paused to look round, and Philip took a seat on some moss while I squatted beside him.

"We'd better build our headquarters here," he announced. "It's a good home base for further excavations."

Philip liked long words, and sometimes read the newspaper in search of them, though he did not always understand them. I had a feeling he did not know what "excavations" actually meant.

"How?" I asked.

"Like a wigwam," explained Philip. "Look, can you see that little mountain ash tree just there? That will be our centre prop. Now we'll collect branches, and lean them up against the middle, close together. Then we'll bind them together with honeysuckle binding, and just leave a little doorway to creep through. We'll have a floor of dead bracken and moss, very soft and comfortable. It will be almost like building a nest. Then, at the back, we'll dig a hole and line it with sticks and stones. We'll bury our supplies there, and cover them with bracken so you won't be able to see anything. It will look just like a floor."

I was thrilled, and set to work immediately. We worked hard all the morning, dragging dead boughs through the undergrowth and cutting long stakes with Philip's clasp knife. Before long we had the skeleton wigwam firmly fixed, with a little doorway just large enough to admit a child – though it was a tight squeeze even for Philip.

It took us some days to complete our wigwam. Every morning, I rushed through my jobs and we made a beeline for the woods. And every morning the pile of dust under the carpet grew bigger and bigger. But, as Aunt Margaret had done the spring cleaning, my laziness was not noticed.

Oh, those mornings in the woods! We seldom kept together. We both wandered off on our own trail, returning to the home base with armfuls of bracken and binding, each of us finding our own treasures and adventures and sharing them on our return.

Perhaps our best find lay in the beech tree just above our wigwam. One day, when I was quietly weaving the wall, I heard a rush of great wings. A brown owl swooped close past me. I was up the trunk in an instant, like an excited squirrel, hoisting myself from branch to branch and searching every hollow and crevice for the nest. My search was rewarded, for there, in the topmost fork of the tree, cradled in straw and fluffy brown feathers lay one pure white egg, hot from the mother's breast.

I climbed down a little way so as not to disturb the mother, and sat swinging my legs and looking about me. The slopes behind the woods were misty with bluebells and, through the thin veil of young green, I caught the glint of kingcups. I was so happy that it almost hurt. And then I saw Philip, looking very small, moving slowly through the trees, his arms full of bracken.

"Phil!" I called. "Come up here!"

He was up in a minute. Together we gazed in deep delight at the pure, precious thing. Then we caught sight of the mother sitting in the next beech, snapping her yellow eyes angrily, and we thought we had better go down. Instantly she spread her great brown pinions and dropped on to her nest. We slid down and discussed baby owls, lying on our tummies in the wigwam.

Everything went well for a week, and Aunt Margaret seemed content enough to let us go our own way. If ever I noticed her looking tired and overworked, I told myself that it was not my business. My holidays were my own. I was going to spend them how I pleased and, in any case, I wasn't much good at housework. So it was rather annoying to me one morning when my aunt stopped me, just as I was tearing out of the house, and asked me where I was going.

"Out with Philip," I answered, wriggling a little under her restraining hand. "I've done my jobs, honestly I have, Aunt Margaret. Please let me go. Phil's waiting for me."

"Well," replied my aunt quietly, "I think Philip must be content to go alone this morning. I need you, Ruth. I've got a big wash this morning, and you can help me in pegging out the clothes and turning the wringer. It's time you did a lot more than you do."

I kicked the ground and looked just about as sullen as it's possible for a child to look.

"But I specially wanted to go out today," I whined.

Aunt Margaret gave me a little shake.

"Well, you can just do what somebody else wants, for a change," she replied. "And if you can't do as you're told cheerfully, you can stay in this afternoon as well. You are getting more lazy and selfish every day. The sooner you take yourself in hand, the better."

She marched off to the kitchen and I followed, scuffling my feet and scowling. I was furious. The owl egg might hatch today, and I should miss it! The blue tits might come out of their nest, and Philip would see them alone. It wasn't fair! I hated Aunt Margaret at that moment, and I made up my mind I wasn't going to help her. I'd be as useless as I could and then she'd be sorry she'd ever asked me to stay.

My thoughts were interrupted by the back door being flung open and Philip's head appearing. He had been working for Uncle Peter in the garden, and looked somewhat flushed and tousled.

"Coming, Ruth?" he asked eagerly.

"No, she's not coming," replied my aunt shortly. "She's going to make herself useful for a change. You run away and play by yourself this morning, Philip. Ruth can join you this afternoon, if she behaves herself."

We both had a miserable morning. I made ugly faces at the table and turned the mangle sullenly. I sighed, and yawned, and scuffed the floor. I kicked the furniture, and scowled at my aunt's back. But she was working hard at the washtub and pretended not to notice. I *knew* she was pretending. She often pretended not to notice my tempers, and nothing annoyed me more. What was the good of being sulky when she would not even look at me? I grew crosser and crosser.

She noticed me all right in the end, however, because she told me to carry out a basin of clean handkerchiefs and hang them on the line. I did not really mean to drop them. But I was so busy slamming the back door and rattling the clothes pegs that the basin slipped from my hands. All the handkerchiefs were scattered in the yard. It had rained in the night, too, and the yard was very muddy.

My aunt was very angry indeed. I think she would have liked to box my ears, for I saw her clasp her hands tightly together. She told me the truth about myself in no uncertain terms and said I might go now, as I was more trouble than I was worth on a busy morning. But she said that for a whole week I was to stay in every morning and work in the house. By the end of that time she hoped I would have learned how to be a little more pleasant and useful, and a little less clumsy. She spoke about my selfishness, and what a disappointment I should be to my mother. Then she took the basin of muddy handkerchiefs out of my hands and went into the house.

I stamped my foot, gulped back my tears, and marched out of the gate with my head in the air. I had lost my mornings for a week, but there was an hour left before dinner. I would go to meet Philip, and walk home with him.

It was a very quiet morning, clouded and hazy and warm after rain. All the world smelt sweet and fresh and fragrant. I felt strangely out of place with my ugly, angry thoughts and my tear-stained face. So much so that I even stopped to think about it, and looked about me. There were the trees quietly doing their work, each leaf perfect in its unfolding, each opening bud a miracle. There was no fret or needless hurry – just the peace of doing something well. I couldn't have put it into words at the time, but that peace seemed to enter into me for a few minutes. I stood thinking how perfect life would be if only I could be good.

I did not often want to be good, but I wanted it then. I wanted with all my heart to be good and happy and useful, in harmony with God's world. I even clasped my hands together and spoke aloud, because I wanted it so badly.

"I want to be good," I said. "I don't want to lose my temper and be selfish. Oh! *Why* can't I be good?"

But my words seemed to float away into the empty air, for at that time I knew nothing of Someone who stood so close to me, longing to help and change me. To me, Jesus was nothing more than a person who had lived long ago, and about whom I read in church. So after a few minutes I shrugged my shoulders and went on.

"I never shall be," I muttered. "I shall always be horrible and cross, and nobody will ever like me."

I met Philip, absolutely beside himself with joy. He did not seem to have missed me at all!

"I watched the egg hatch," he announced. "I went up and the mother flew off. When I looked, the shell was cracked and I could see the membrane heaving up and down. I daren't stay in case it got cold and the owlet died. The mother's back now, brooding on it. I shouldn't go up if I were you, because she might peck you."

There wasn't time to go up, in any case, as it was time to go home to dinner. On the way, I told Philip of my tragic morning. He was comforting and sympathetic, and I felt better, even though I knew perfectly well that I deserved no sympathy. Then, in his own thoughtful way, he stopped talking about the mornings and we spent the rest of our walk home planning the afternoons.

# 3

# Terry

It was only three days later that we had our first adventure and made a new friend. This is how it happened.

The wigwam was well and truly finished and as snug a little house as anyone could wish, with its secret hiding place where we hid our tea and other belongings when we went exploring. The blue tits had left the nest. We had watched their first uncertain flight, and had seen them flounder on to the moss, screaming for their mother. The owlet, too, was growing. He now resembled a ball of soft grey cotton wool, with a hooked beak and round yellow eyes.

This particular afternoon the wind was behind us, blowing strongly from the hills. We had been caught up in it and had run all the way. Being carried along like that had made us laugh. We reached the wigwam quite breathless with running and laughter, ready to fling ourselves down on the mossy floor and recover our breath in the cool, dark shade of its walls. So it was quite a shock to me when Philip, who had dived halfway through the entrance, suddenly backed out on to his haunches, his eyes wide with astonishment.

He whispered dramatically, "The wigwam is occupied!"

"Who by?" I asked indignantly, backing a step or two.

"Well, I couldn't exactly see," replied Philip, "but I think it's a boy."

"Well," I said loudly, "it's *our* wigwam, and he'd better come out, because we want to go in."

There was a dead silence.

"You'd better come out!" said Philip, very loudly and clearly.

Still no answer.

"Perhaps it's a dead body?" I suggested.

"No it isn't," answered Philip. "I saw it scratch itself."

There was a long, uncertain silence. Philip began to giggle.

"I think I'd better go in and look again," he said. "Perhaps he can't hear us."

He went down on all fours and approached the entrance with extreme caution. His front half disappeared into the doorway, and another long silence ensued.

"Hurry up!" I exclaimed impatiently, taking hold of his back legs in my excitement. "Who is he? And what is he doing?"

"We're just staring," said Philip with another giggle. "It's a boy, as I said." He spoke to the visitor. "This is *our* wigwam, and we're coming in, so you'd better get out."

"Shan't!" said a voice from within.

"Then I shall pull you out," said Philip.

"Then I shall catch hold o' the wall and pull it down with me," answered the voice coolly.

Another silence, while, I guessed, the rivals eyed each other stubbornly. I danced up and down with excitement and indignation.

Philip broke the silence.

"I know," he said, "let's have a tournament, like in the history book!"

"A how much?" asked the voice. Its owner seemed unfamiliar with history books.

"A tournament," repeated Philip. "It's like a fight between two people who are having a quarrel. Whoever wins the fight wins the quarrel. You come out and fight, and if I win you go away, but if you win you can share the wigwam. Because, after all, you know, we *did* build it."

Our uninvited visitor seemed to like this idea, for I saw Philip wriggle out of the entrance backwards and roll over on to the ground, so making room for him to come out. And, angry as I was, the minute I saw our visitor's face in the gap I liked him, and wanted to know him.

I hope Philip wins, I thought to myself. But all the same, I hope this boy will stay and play. I like him.

He was a little boy, about as big as me, but he looked around the same age as Philip. His clothes were ragged and rather too small for him. But his eyes were as bright as a blackbird's, and his face was tanned and powdered with freckles. His thick hair fell down over his forehead, and reminded me of an untidy thatch. In his arms he held an enormous bunch of kingcups and cowslips. He laid them carefully on the moss and told me to let 'em alone while he knocked out "this posh kid".

The tournament began in a highly irregular fashion, before anyone was ready for it, for the boy suddenly ran at Philip and punched him on the jaw. Philip, taken by surprise, hadn't the time to hit back before he was punched again on the ear. Even then he stood and blinked several times before making up his mind what to do about it.

"*Hit* him, Phil!" I yelled, nearly joining in myself, and beating the nearest tree to relieve my feelings.

It was a good fight to watch, once Philip got started. Philip was as strong and as determined as an ox, but the other boy reminded me of a little ferret. He twisted and turned, and leaped and wriggled, his tanned arms bulging with muscle, and his lips pressed tightly together. Back he came, time and again, while Philip stood his ground and measured out slow, relentless blows. It was a very exciting tournament indeed, and I behaved like a whole gallery of spectators rolled into one.

The boy won. He pretended to spring at Philip's neck, and then suddenly changed his tactics, and dived between his feet, bringing my brother to the ground with an alarming crash. By the time Philip had realised what was happening, the boy was sitting on his chest, thumping him with all his might.

"Stop it!" said Philip. "You've won."

"Beat yer 'ollow!" said the boy, getting up. "But I don't want yer silly ol' hut. I could build a better one meself."

He was gathering up his flowers and making off, when Philip ran over to him and held him by the braces.

"Don't go!" he said. "We'd quite like you to share the wigwam, and then perhaps one day we'll have another fight. I love fighting, don't you?"

"It's not bad," said the boy.

"We're going to have tea now," urged Philip. "Come and have it with us. There's room for all three inside."

It was not nearly teatime really, but we both felt we must do something to hang on to the boy, and at the word "tea", a remarkable change came over him. He stopped looking sullen and bored, and suddenly became interested. Without even troubling to say "Yes", he squatted down on the moss with an expectant smile on his face, and held out his grubby hand.

He must have been terribly hungry, for I had never seen anyone eat at such a speed. We opened our packet of sandwiches and, without so much as a "Please" or "Thank you", he fell upon them and finished three while Philip and I were still eating our first. Then, when the last crumb had disappeared and he had licked the jam off the paper, he gave a sigh of relief and we all settled down to get to know each other.

We lay on our tummies, our faces cupped in our hands, and the bluebells tickling our chins pleasantly. The afternoon sun came slanting through the trees in golden bars and made leaf-shadow patterns on the ground. Up above, the wind murmured in the tree tops. But we were sheltered and warm and peaceful.

"What's your name?" asked Philip.

"Terry," the boy replied, and went on chewing a piece of grass.

"How old are you?"

"Eleven come August."

"Where do you live?"

"At the cottage in the 'ollow by the stream down Tanglewoods way."

"Have you any brothers and sisters?"

"No – there's only me and Mum."

"Where's your father?"

"'Aven't got none."

"What are all those flowers for?"

"Me mum sells 'em in the town – she's a flower seller."

"Do you pick them all for her?"

"Yes, when I can cut school."

Nobody spoke for a time. Then I suddenly had an idea. I put my hand on his arm.

"Would you like to see an owl's nest?" I asked.

For an answer he pointed upwards to the tree. "That one?" he asked. "I've seen 'im once today. That nest was 'ere last year too."

I felt a little bit annoyed. It was *our* owl's nest, and he had no business to get there first. But Philip was before me. He leaned eagerly over towards the boy.

"Do you know lots of nests?" he asked. "Could you show us any more?"

Terry looked at us rather scornfully.

"I could show yer just about every nest in this 'ere wood," he replied.

Philip jumped to his feet. "Come on!" he cried. "Let's go and see! Show us them all, Terry!"

Terry got up slowly and looked us up and down, as though making up his mind as to whether we were the sort of children to be trusted with nests. Then he nodded.

"Right!" he answered briefly, and dived into the bushes.

A breathless hour followed, at the end of which I was quite exhausted and nearly torn to pieces, for Terry never stopped at an obstacle. We waded knee-deep in a pond to inspect a reed warbler's woven home, and we swarmed impossible trees in search of crows' nests. We inspected holes in trunks, and watched a starling fly in and out. The wood was opened up to us, and we found out more about it in that hour than ever before. The sun was setting when we turned home.

"Goodbye," we said, and then we hesitated. Must this be the end? Would such a fun boy want to see us again?

"Coming again?" said Terry casually, and we heaved a great sigh of relief. From that moment Terry was our friend. And, better still, we knew that he looked on us as his friends.

# 4

# The lost lamb

We saw Terry nearly every day after that and the time passed only too quickly. He led us all over the countryside and showed us his secret nests and lairs and burrows. We learned to identify and track the footprints of little animals, and to recognise the different cries of birds and what they meant. He dragged us through swamps and marshes and brambles in search of the earliest flowers, and showed us where to gather rare orchids. It was as though he had opened up to us a new world of wonder, and we both liked and admired him for his amazing knowledge of woodland life. Before, I had always disliked Philip's friends, because I thought they took him away from me. But Terry seemed to think us both equally his friends, even though I was younger.

So it was a disappointment to us all when Philip twisted his ankle while swinging from a tree and, after hobbling home, had to lie on a couch till it got better.

I stayed at home to help amuse Philip. I believe my efforts were quite successful, but they nearly drove Aunt Margaret crazy. I started by catching a duck and bringing it in, dressed up in a doll's bonnet, to call on the invalid. Then I let the duck loose on the dining room carpet. We forgot it after a little while. It waddled out into the passage, where it met my aunt, who was *not* pleased to see it. We heard the duck being shown out of the front door in a great hurry, squawking angrily. We watched it waddling across the lawn, the pink silk bonnet turning from side to side as the duck looked about.

Next day, we decided to play toy soldiers. I settled myself at the other end of the dining room from Philip's couch. We had a whole army and a dozen marbles each. We bombed each other quite happily for a time, till it suddenly struck us that the kittens in the woodshed would make excellent army cavalry. So off I trotted, returning with an armful of soft, purring, black and tabby fur, which I dropped on the floor. Four blue-eyed kittens with twitching tails and whiskers sorted themselves out and rushed into corners.

I selected a tabby and a black and white one, and Philip had two coal-blacks to represent his army. We let fire on the leaden infantry, and then the cavalry charge began.

It was a marvellous game, and the kittens loved it. They tore after the marbles in all directions, slaughtering the soldiers right and left. Philip and I shrieked with laughter. We both rushed round on all fours collecting our ammunition and recapturing the cavalry. Faster and faster ran the kittens, fiercer and fiercer grew the battle, when suddenly there was a crash and a splash. The tabby had leaped on to a dangling tablecloth and pulled it, together with a vase of flowers, over on top of himself. Of course, at that moment the door opened and Aunt Margaret came in.

The kittens instantly rushed between her feet. One stopped and dug his tiny claws into her stocking. The naughty tabby, unable to disentangle himself, rolled over and over all wrapped up in the tablecloth. The flower water streamed across the carpet, and Philip and I lay flat on the floor and laughed until the tears ran down our cheeks.

My aunt was not amused. I will not describe the scene that followed. But it finished up with four very excited little kittens being banished to the woodshed again, and one very cross little girl being turned out of the house as Philip was given a book, and put back on the couch.

I spent the next ten minutes or so sitting on the woodpile sulking. It wasn't fair! Aunt Margaret had said it was all my fault, but it had been Philip's fault just as much as mine *that* time, so I told myself. I had actually suggested the kittens, but Philip had thought it a good idea. And, anyhow, why *shouldn't* we play together? I didn't like being sent off alone like that. I hated Aunt Margaret. The more I thought about it, the more I thought it wasn't me who wrecked things at all, it was the kittens. At that point I suddenly thought of that wet tabby rolling round inside the tablecloth. I began to giggle, and felt better.

I got up and went over to smell some early lilies of the valley that were coming out by the wall. By this time I was quite happy again. After all, it was very nice to be out of doors on a sunny spring day, even if I was alone. I decided to go to the woods and see if I could find Terry anywhere. So I squeezed through the gap in the hedge and strolled off.

I didn't go far into the woods, for the sun was pleasant on the outskirts and I wanted to pick flowers. The bracken was already beginning to shoot up and hide the bluebells, but the vetches were rambling over the ditches, and orchids and woodruff grew in the clearings.

So I wandered round, thinking of Philip and Terry, and Mother, and nests, and the far away hills, and bluebells, and wigwams, until I had almost forgotten where I was. It gave me quite a surprise to hear a man's voice quite close to me.

I looked up quickly, but he was not calling me. He was standing with his back to me, peering into the thickets. He had not seen me at all. But I recognised him at once. It was Mr Tandy, the Cradley shepherd who had picked up the orphan lamb and carried it under his coat.

Being rather an inquisitive child, I wanted to know what he was doing, so I went and stood where he could see me. As soon as he caught sight of me, he smiled broadly.

"Well, well!" he exclaimed. "You're the little maid as played with the lamb t'other day, and here you are a-turning up again just at the right moment. One of the little rascals 'as strayed, and I'm thinking as how he's caught somewhere here in these bushes, but I can't just see where. Maybe you'll stop and help find him."

I was only too delighted. Here was something nice to do, and a pleasant companion to do it with, so I set to work at once. I liked this old man with his white hair and his rosy face, and I felt he liked me. We were soon talking away as though we had known each other all our lives.

"Why did he stray?" I asked, as we parted the bushes and searched the ditches.

"Well," answered the old man, with a smile, "I reckon he's just like the rest of us. He likes his own way, and his own way's led him into trouble, poor little chap!"

"Well," I remarked, "I expect he's sorry for it now – all tied up in the bushes, and wishing he'd stayed in his meadow."

"Aye," agreed Mr Tandy, thoughtfully. "It often takes thorns and briers to teach them lambs as their own way isn't the best one. He'll be crying his heart out for me now, if only I could find the place."

"Won't he be glad to see us!" I observed. "Oh! I'm longing to find him! I expect he'll be very tired and hungry. Have you anything for him to eat?"

He put his hand into his pocket, and drew out a bottle.

"You'll see!" he said. "The minute I pick him up in my arms, he'll have his nose in my pocket. He knows I wouldn't forget 'im... the little rascal!"

He chuckled softly, and we moved further into the wood.

"He's strayed a long way, hasn't he?" I remarked.

"True," answered Mr Tandy, "but I'll find him yet. I've never yet had a lamb go astray, but that I've found them and brought them home. I always hear them crying out somewhere or other, although at times 'tis a long search."

"What's the longest you've ever searched for?" I asked.

"'Most one night," he replied, "but that was in a storm, and I could scarce hear her cryings for the wind and the thunder. She was caught fast in a bramble bush, and I found her at dawn by lantern light. She was almost dead with cold and hunger and crying."

"And what did you do?"

"Do?" repeated Mr Tandy. "Why, I set her free and quietened her, and wrapped her in my coat, and carried her home. She was like a wild thing when we found her, but once she felt my arms round her she lay as quiet as a baby. She knew there was nothing more to be a-feared of then!"

I was about to ask another question, but he suddenly held up his hand and stood perfectly still, listening.

I had heard nothing, but his practised shepherd's ear had caught the sound at once – the faint cry of a tired lamb calling for help.

"That'll be him," he said simply, "in those bushes." And he made straight for the sound.

It was a wonder to me, when we saw him, how the little creature had ever got in, the hedge was so matted and the briers so thick. And it was a still greater wonder to me that the shepherd ever got him out of that thorn bush. But we started off, parting the boughs, and as he worked he spoke to the lamb as a mother might speak to a frightened little child.

I don't suppose the lamb understood the words, but he knew the voice in an instant – knew in a flash that he was sought and found and loved. At the sound of the shepherd's voice, he ceased his weak struggles and fretful crying. He gave one joyful bleat and then lay still and waited.

It took a long time to reach him. I stood and watched while the old man patiently worked at the tangle, thorn by thorn, and brier by brier. When he finally picked up the little runaway, his hands were dreadfully scratched and bleeding, but he didn't seem to notice. He just held that trembling lamb close and let it nuzzle its black nose trustfully into his pocket.

"Are ye ready to come home?" he whispered, playfully lifting the little smudged face to his own.

"Baaa!" said the lamb, and then put its nose back into the shepherd's pocket.

We walked home quietly, the lamb lying in the crook of his arm. Mr Tandy seemed to be thinking deeply and his face looked very happy. I longed to share his thoughts, but did not like to ask, so I said nothing.

When we reached the meadow, the sun was setting and the sky behind the bluebell slopes was the colour of pink shells. We laid the lamb among the others, and he gave a bleat of content and fell fast asleep.

'"Well," I said slowly, "I suppose I'd better be getting home now. Thank you for letting me help. I hope I'll see you again soon."

But Mr Tandy asked me to sit down beside him on the wooden bench that ran round the outside of the fold. "Before you go, little maid," he said, "I'll read you a bit of a story about another sheep as strayed." And as he spoke, he took a small, worn New Testament from his pocket, and opened it at Luke, chapter 15. Then he began to read, in his slow, kind, country voice.

I suppose I had heard the story before, but it had never interested me. But now it was different. It seemed to belong to the sloping buttercup fields, and the long evening shadows and the pink sky, and the sleeping folded sheep. I listened with all my heart as Mr Tandy spoke about the lost sheep, and the shepherd who went looking for it.

"If any of you has a hundred sheep, and one of them gets lost, what will you do? Won't you leave the ninety-nine in the field and go and look for the lost sheep until you find it? And when you find it, you will be so glad that you will put it on your shoulder and carry it home. Then you will call in your friends and neighbours and say, 'Let's celebrate! I've found my lost sheep.'… In the same way there is more happiness in heaven because of one sinner who turns to God than over ninety-nine good people who don't need to."

He closed his Testament, and I looked up at him.

"Goodnight, little maid," he said.

"Goodnight," I answered, "and thank you very much." And I walked slowly home through the buttercups.

# 5

# A brilliant idea

I never told Philip about the shepherd. At least, not about that last bit. I was afraid he would laugh and think it odd, and I should not have liked that. In any case, I almost forgot about it next day, because I had one of my brainwaves, and when I had a brainwave I could never think of anything else until I had carried it out.

It came about next day, when Philip was hobbling round the garden, not yet being able to walk to the woods. We had played all our usual games, and were lying under the apple trees wondering what to do next. As there wasn't anything much to do, we just lay and chatted, and Philip started talking about his book again.

"It's getting very fat, Ruth," he assured me, "and it's full of useful information about birds. All I'm waiting for now is the camera to take the pictures. I shan't get it for years. Just think," he went on dreamily, "what a beautiful picture that baby owl would have made. And those blue tits sitting in a row on the hawthorn bush."

"Never mind," I said comfortingly, "we've got quite a bit more than when we last counted, so we're getting on!"

"But it's so slow," sighed Philip. "I shall soon be nearly grown up, and I expect I shall be sent to boarding school, and there won't be much chance to take pictures. I wish Auntie would let me be an errand boy, and earn something in my spare time."

I interrupted his thoughts by suddenly pouncing on him and slapping him violently on the back.

"Philip!" I shouted. "I've had a brilliant idea!"

"What is it?" he asked, doubtfully. He was a little suspicious of my good ideas. They so often turned out badly, and ended up with punishments.

"It really is a good idea this time, Philip," I grinned, "and Aunt Margaret could never discover it. We'll pick flowers, like Terry's mother does, and sell them! We'll earn pounds and pounds. Do say yes, Phil! It would be such fun!"

Philip was still extremely doubtful.

"But Terry's mother wouldn't like it," he objected, "because if they bought our flowers, they wouldn't buy hers as well, and then she wouldn't get so much money."

"Oh, but we shan't go to the same places," I assured him. "She sells hers in the street in the town. We'll go to people's back doors, and we'll dress up a bit to look like gypsies."

Philip's eyes danced. He was coming round to my idea, as I knew he would sooner or later.

"Let's go to the big houses halfway up the hill, where they have big iron gates and drives," he said. "We'll dress up in our oldest clothes like gypsy children. We'll make our faces a bit dirty and wear our muddiest shoes. You tie your plaits up in your red hanky, and we'll get pounds and pounds and *pounds*. Let's start soon!"

I always liked to carry out all my plans instantly, and leaped to my feet immediately. Then I remembered Philip's ankle, and tried to curb my impatience.

"You'll be able to walk tomorrow, won't you?" I pleaded. "Although, even if you couldn't, a little limp would be quite helpful. It would make people sorry for you. We could say, 'Pity the poor lame beggar!' and you could put a big white hanky round your ankle and look as though it hurt you. Only you wouldn't have to do it too much, because it would make me laugh."

I laughed delightedly at the very thought, and rolled about joyfully in the grass.

Philip's ankle was much better next day, and we escaped early and made for the woods with a big wicker shopping basket. We were going to pick all the morning and sell all the afternoon. We had no idea of prices, which rather worried us, but we were trusting to luck rather than to judgement, and hoped for the best.

"Where are you going?" I asked Philip, as we reached the stile.

"Down to the swamp in the hollow," he replied. "I'm going to pick lots of cowslips, and there are some late kingcups out, and the valerian's in bud. I might find some orchids, too, to put in with the cowslips. The colours go well together."

"We can get some wild cherry blossom, too," I added, "and I'm going to pick little bunches of wood sorrel and violets for tiny pots. We'll sell them cheaply to the people who don't want big bunches. Oh, Phil! What fun it will be!"

I was dancing down the sloping path that led to the swamp, and nearly collided with a swinging bough of cherry blossom swaying low across the path. I stopped to pick some, and Philip caught me up. He did not help me, but stood quietly staring up at the pure clusters.

"Isn't it beautiful?" he remarked slowly. "It's like great snowdrifts up there."

"Yes," I answered absently. "Pick some, Philip! I'm doing all the work."

"Isn't it a pity," went on Philip, taking no notice of me, "that it doesn't last? It will all have fallen in a few days, and the blossom will be all brown and ugly. Nothing beautiful really lasts, does it?"

"Oh, there'll be some bird cherries later on, I expect," I answered, in a matter-of-fact voice. "Stop staring, Philip! It's silly to think about things like that. Get on and pick some flowers."

Philip stooped down and started gathering large late violets but his blue eyes were serious. I marched on rather crossly, for I didn't like Philip in these melancholy moods. But although I tried to forget them, his last words kept ringing in my ears: "Nothing beautiful really lasts, does it?"

It was quite true. All the nasty things like tempers and rows with Aunt Margaret went on and on, and you couldn't get rid of them. They might stop for a time, but you knew they would always come back. But beautiful things like holidays, and blossom, and sunsets, and birds singing, faded and died and left you empty. Certainly other beautiful things came and took their places, but they didn't comfort you for the ones that had gone.

"Not one single thing," I said aloud to Philip, who had caught me up.

"Not one single what?" asked my brother vaguely.

"Beautiful thing lasting," I explained, frowning.

"Oh!" said Philip. "No, I suppose not, but it doesn't really matter, because more come."

"Yes, but those new things... Philip, are you listening?" Then I saw the reason why he had become suddenly distracted. He had seen a jay.

"Jays usually nest low down," he said. "So keep your eyes open."

I sighed, quite familiar with my brother's obsession. Anyway, we had nearly reached the swamp now, so we turned our serious attention to the flowers.

We picked hard all the morning, and quite filled the shopping basket with our bunches. There were golden balls of cowslips mixed with vivid purple orchids and lacy white woodruff. The dazzling brightness of the buttercups we veiled with cow parsley, and mingled the kingcups with cotton grass and valerian. The blossom we left by itself, for we felt that its perfect whiteness was best unadorned. I carried it separately, while Philip carried the basket. We hid all our flowers in the orchard, and went in to dinner, inwardly bubbling over with excitement, but outwardly quite calm.

Aunt Margaret looked rather hard at Philip, who was gobbling his dinner at a tremendous pace. She was a little suspicious of our wanting to be off again so quickly.

"Philip," she said rather severely, "I think you should rest that ankle this afternoon. You've done enough walking on it this morning."

Philip turned injured blue eyes upon her.

"Oh, Auntie," he assured her, in his most polite voice, "I've been standing still nearly all the morning. I just went to the swamp and stayed there and picked a few flowers. I think, too," he added seriously, "that a lot of exercise makes my ankle feel better. It stops it getting stiff. In fact, I had planned to walk on it as much as possible this afternoon."

And Philip, as usual, had his way, as he always did with my aunt.

"Very well," she agreed, "but don't overdo it – and keep out of that swamp. Your sister's shoes are a perfect disgrace."

Philip looked at my shoes and sighed. He, of course, had remembered to change his before Aunt Margaret noticed them. I, of course, had not. How calm life would be, I thought rather bitterly, if I had been born like Philip!

Aunt Margaret went into the kitchen to wash up after dinner. She did not ask me to help her, and I certainly did not offer. I was always full of excuses and arguments when asked to help, and my aunt was rather tired today, so she did not bother me.

Once the door was firmly closed, I fled upstairs. I untwisted my plaits and my hair fell dark and loose to my waist. Then I tied up my head in my big handkerchief that Mother had sent me from India, and put on a dirty pinafore. My muddy shoes needed no touching up. I looked like a little wild urchin. Philip in his old coat and Wellington boots looked a fit companion for me.

"Don't let Aunt Margaret see us," he whispered cautiously, as we slipped out of the door. "She'll go crazy! We'd better go through the gap."

We climbed the hill that led to the big houses rather slowly, for the day was hot and the basket was heavy. Also I knew that Philip's ankle hurt quite a bit, although he would not admit it. What really worried us was the fact that the flowers were drooping so. Of course, we should have put them in water overnight, but we had been too impatient to wait till next day. Yet, in spite of our impatience, when we actually reached the first pair of iron double gates we seemed in no hurry to go in.

"What are you going to say?" asked Philip, rather nervously.

"Me?" I replied indignantly. "I'm not going to say anything. You've got to say it. You're much better at all that sort of thing than me."

"Oh, well," said Philip, shrugging his shoulders, "perhaps we shan't have to say anything. Perhaps the person who lives here will come to the door and say, 'What beautiful bunches of flowers! I'll buy two.' Then we shall just smile and hand them over, and she'll give us some money and we'll go away."

This charming prospect cheered us up a lot, and we walked rather quicker until the path divided. The left hand path ran round the front between beautiful lawns, flowerbeds and cedar trees. The right hand one ran around to the back.

"Do we go front or back?" I asked.

"Back, I think," said Philip. "After all, we mustn't forget we're gypsies."

Our timid knock at the back door sounded dreadfully loud, so loud that we both jumped. We had hardly had time to recover ourselves before the door was flung open and a housemaid appeared. She was a very grand housemaid with a big nose and bright red lips and dyed hair set in a permanent wave, and there was a heavy smell of scent about her.

"Well?" she asked, sharply.

It all happened so suddenly that we were both quite taken aback, and simply looked at each other. There was a moment's silence, then a violent desire to scream with laughter seized me. I could *not* speak. I turned away from Philip with shaking shoulders, but not before I had seen that he was feeling as bad as I was. He whisked out his handkerchief and pretended to sneeze into it, but the result was a sort of cross between a snore and a roar, which set me off worse than ever. The tears streamed down my cheeks and I turned my back on the housemaid.

"Well?" she asked again. This time she sounded downright angry, so Philip controlled himself and answered in a very shaky voice.

"Would you like to buy some flowers?" he said in a quivering voice.

"Good gracious, no!" replied the girl. "What in the world should we be buying flowers for here? Didn't you see the gardens? The mistress has more flowers than she knows what to do with. Besides, those what you've got in the basket are all dead."

"Oh, they'll be all right in water..." I began, but she had already slammed the door in our faces, and we were left giggling feebly on the steps.

I wiped my eyes on my pinafore, because I had forgotten my handkerchief. We made off down the drive between beautiful beds of lilies of the valley and wallflowers which we had been too excited to notice on the way up. We kept collapsing in peals of laughter, and were too amused to feel disappointed. Anyhow, we were sure we should be more fortunate next door. Next door could not possibly have someone who looked so silly answering the door, so I would be able to keep a straight face this time.

The next house looked less grand. The garden was smaller, and we could see the front door from the road. We stopped for a minute to read the notice on the gate. It said "NO HAWKERS, NO CIRCULARS" in large capital letters.

"What does that mean?" I asked.

"I don't know," answered Philip. "It sounds like a man who sells hawks. Anyhow, it couldn't mean us, so come on!"

We walked purposefully up the path, holding the basket between us.

"Whatever happens, we mustn't laugh this time," said Philip. "Don't let's look at each other at all. Let's just both talk fast, and we shall be all right. And let's go to the front door, because perhaps the masters and mistresses will be nicer than the maids."

We climbed a flight of stone steps, and I pulled the bell handle rather harder than I meant to. It rang so loudly that Philip put his hands over his ears and went quite pale. It seemed awful to have made such a noise on such a quiet afternoon. We gave each other a desperate look, and at that moment the door opened. An elderly lady with an eye-glass and a very straight back stood looking down at us as though she didn't like us much.

We were so determined to have no awkward pauses or chances to giggle that we both started talking at once, very fast and loud.

"We've picked some flowers," said Philip.

"And we thought you might like to buy them," I said.

"They are about six pence, I think," said Philip.

"Unless you think it's too much," I said.

"They look a bit dead," added Philip.

"But they'll be quite all right when you put them in water," I said.

"Because they are really quite fresh," said Philip.

"We only picked them today," I said.

During this surprising flood of conversation, the old lady stood staring at us in indignant astonishment. She took no notice of the withered bunch of cowslips that I was feverishly trying to push into her hand, and asked in an icy voice,

"Little boy and girl, did you not read the notice on the gate?"

"Yes," admitted Philip, rather puzzled, "but I'm not a hawker."

"And I'm sure I'm not a circular," I chimed in, rather pertly.

"Little boy and girl," went on the old lady in a severe voice, "if you are too young to understand the English language, you are certainly too young to be doing this sort of thing. Go home to your mother!"

And for the second time that day we found ourselves standing on the steps with the door shut in our faces.

Philip was discouraged, and suggested going home. But I was more persevering, and urged him on.

"Let's try again!" I pleaded. "They can't all be as nasty as this. Look, this next gate says nothing about circulars, so it must be all right."

"Neither did the first one," murmured Philip, but he followed me inside. We set off up the drive, the basket apparently growing heavier and the day growing hotter every minute.

There was a beautiful rock garden on one side of the drive. I was walking a little ahead when I suddenly noticed a clump of brilliant bell gentians nestling in a crevice. Never before had I seen such a heavenly blue. In an instant, I had squatted down to examine them more closely. I didn't realise it at the time but at the same moment, Philip, trudging along behind me, saw a skylark soar upwards and remain poised and motionless. He threw his head back and walked on, forgetful of everything else and, of course, tripped right over me, head first. I rolled over, with my legs waving wildly, the basket fell and scattered the flowers in all directions, and we both screamed at the top of our voices.

It was at this point that a man came round the corner, and nearly fell over us as well.

"What on earth...!" he began, but by this time we had sorted ourselves out, and were sitting up.

"Sorry!" said Philip, rubbing his nose.

"You tripped over me," I remarked indignantly.

"Well, you shouldn't have squatted down like that," protested Philip.

"Well, you shouldn't have had your head in the air!" I argued.

"Well, I was watching a skylark," explained my brother, "and, oh, listen! I can hear it now!"

"Are you interested in birds?" asked the man suddenly.

"Yes," replied Philip, coming out of his dream and lifting serious blue eyes to his questioner. "Are you?"

"Very," answered the man. "I have all sorts of birds nesting in this garden. I'll show you some if you get up... unless you and your sister – I take it this *is* your sister? – wish to sit in the middle of the drive all the afternoon."

Philip jumped to his feet and walked away with the man. I gathered up the flowers and followed. They were already deep in conversation on the subject of goldcrests.

We had a very happy half hour, for the man showed us four or five rare nests, and Philip was delighted. Then, when we had been all round the garden, the man took us on to the veranda and gave us each a drink of lemonade. And, as we drank it, he suddenly remarked, "By the way, why did you come?"

Philip had quite forgotten our real errand, and looked quite startled for a moment. So I answered for him, holding out the basket.

"We came to sell flowers," I explained, "but we fell over. Would you like to buy some?"

The man selected three bunches of withered cowslips.

"Is this how you earn your living?" he asked gravely.

"Oh, no," I replied, "not really. We wanted to earn some money for something special, so we thought we'd sell some flowers. But nobody seems to want them."

"Nonsense!" said the man. "Cowslips are my favourite flowers. I'd pay a lot for a scent like that." And he pressed several coins into my hand.

Philip went rather red. Then he said earnestly, "We should like to give them to you. You have given us such a lovely afternoon, and… and… we are very much obliged to you."

The last words came out with a rush, as though he was reading a speech. The man's eyes twinkled, but he spoke gravely.

"Not at all," he replied. "It's been a pleasure to meet you, and I should like your little sister to keep all the money. You have an extraordinary knowledge of birds for one so young, and I should like you to come again."

I put the coins in my pocket in a great hurry. I was dreadfully afraid the man would take Philip at his word, but he didn't. He walked to the gate with us, and we all shook hands and said, "Thank you." Then he turned back up the drive and we stood, once again, in the road.

"Let's go home," said Philip.

"All right," I agreed. "We didn't do badly for a first day, and we can try again tomorrow."

But Philip did not answer. He was walking down the road in a happy dream. I knew that he had been in paradise.

# 6

# An unfortunate tea party

We went out flower selling nearly every afternoon after that, for a week, and earned 75 pence. We never again met anyone quite so nice as the bird man, but quite a lot of people seemed pleased with our flowers and bought bunches. They looked better now, too, because we remembered to put them in a bucket of water overnight instead of selling them at once. The basket of fresh, wild bunches made a good show.

We took Terry into our confidence, and he did not mind at all. In fact, he helped us quite a lot, for he had a gift of selecting the right colours and arranging them to perfection. In order that Aunt Margaret should not see the flowers, we kept the bucket by the gap in the hedge. Terry would sometimes arrive there late in the evenings and add a few of his finds to ours. We had shown him our private gap as a mark of friendship, and he used to creep in and out like a small weasel, and leave notes for us, stuck on the apple boughs. His spelling was shaky, but that did not worry us at all. Anyhow, we had invented a code, in case Uncle Peter ever found the notes when attending to the hens. Aunt Margaret we felt quite safe about. She never went into the orchard.

Most mornings we found a scrap of paper which said, "Cum to A – bring ooooo." This meant that Terry would be waiting for us at the wigwam, and would require feeding. And where Terry commanded, we always obeyed. Aunt Margaret almost gave up the struggle of trying to make me help in the house, and I became really gifted at getting out of doing my jobs. If I ever had a twinge of conscience about her tired and rather sad face, I managed to forget it the minute I had dived through the gap in the hedge and was out in the world again.

At the end of the week, when we were sitting at dinner, my aunt remarked,

"I'm going out to tea this afternoon, Philip and Ruth, and I shan't be back till about six. You may have your tea outside, and not come back till supper, if you like."

We both *did* like, very much, and we kicked each other joyfully under the table.

"Who are you going out to tea with, Auntie?" asked Philip, who always took a polite interest in other people's affairs.

"With an old friend of mine who has come to live here just lately," answered my aunt. "Later on, I should like to introduce you to her. She is very fond of children, and has often asked about you. She knows your mother, too."

"Will she ask us out to tea, as well?" I said with interest. I liked going out to tea because we always had such nice things to eat.

"If she did, you would have to behave yourself rather better than you usually do," replied my aunt dryly, and I frowned and wriggled with annoyance. Why should she always spoil even nice, good things like going out to tea, with silly remarks like that? Of course I always behaved nicely when I went out to tea! I was far too shy not to and, in any case, it was rather fun having grown-ups say how well-mannered Philip and I were... quite a change, too, as far as I was concerned.

Dinner over, my aunt carried me off to the kitchen to help dry up the dishes, which I did at lightning speed, and made off the instant I'd finished. Aunt Margaret called after me to come back and put the cloth away tidily. But I pretended not to hear, and scuttled through the front door. I knew she could not possibly catch me, for I was as fast as a little rabbit, and I hoped she might have forgotten by the evening. Going out to tea would drive it out of her memory.

Philip was waiting near the gap, looking rather anxious, with the basket in his hand.

"Come on," he said, "we must get well away before Auntie starts. We might meet her, and we forgot to ask which way she was going."

"Oh, I think she's going down the town way," I answered carelessly. "I heard her say something to Uncle Peter about it – someone she was going to see down Beech Road."

"But perhaps she meant somebody else," objected Philip.

"No, no," I replied reassuringly, "it was sure to be the same person. She doesn't go and see many people. She's too busy."

Philip chewed a piece of grass thoughtfully.

"She's always working, isn't she?" he remarked at last. "Sometimes I think we might help her a bit more than we do. After all, it's quite kind of her to have us to live with her. We're not her children."

"Oh, I don't know," I answered quickly, for this sort of talk was not at all to my liking. "I help with the drying and dusting sometimes, and you do the wood for Uncle Peter, and we both pick fruit in summer, and shell peas and things. After all, we're not grown-ups, and children shouldn't have to work in the holidays. We do quite enough work in the term."

But I could see by the look on Philip's face that he was not quite satisfied, so I changed the subject as soon as possible.

We went down a country road that day, to a collection of rather pretty cottages mostly inhabited by retired, elderly ladies. The may was beginning to come out, and the boughs of the hedges were weighed down with the heavy blossom. Underneath, on the banks, buttercups, vetches, dead nettles, speedwells and cow parsley grew in sweet-scented riot, all stretching up towards the sunshine. It was the high tide of late spring, and the birds sang as though they would burst their throats with song. It was a peaceful sort of day on which no one would expect anything to happen. So we were taken completely by surprise, never dreaming that the afternoon would turn out as it did.

The old ladies were unusually nice, too, and at the first four cottages everyone bought something, and we earned over twenty pence. I had noticed that most old ladies fell in love with Philip and did whatever he wanted. I suppose it was his blue eyes and his polite, serious way of speaking. Today, one of them patted him on the head and called him "Little man", which he did not like at all, and one of them gave us a chocolate each, which we liked very much indeed.

We wandered up a lane to have tea, and sat on a gate looking over a radiant buttercup field, where sleepy brown cows chewed their cud and switched their tails lazily. We munched our bread and jam as peacefully as the cows and almost as silently, for Philip was not really a talkative boy.

He had a good deal to think about, as he sometimes told me when I chattered more than he liked.

Tea finished, we lay down in the grass. Then, as it was still only four o'clock, we decided to go back to the road and try some more cottages. We were going to do our best today, and then go back to Terry and the woods tomorrow, for we were getting a little tired of flower selling. Still, it was encouraging to be finishing up so well and, on reaching the road, we approached the next cottage hopefully.

It was a very nice one, long, low and built of grey stone, with beds of tulips massed against it. It stood on a little rise, and a pink and white apple orchard sloped away from one side of it. We pattered up the path and along to the front door. On our way we passed by a window, and heard the clink of china and the sound of ladies' voices. It sounded as if some sort of a tea party was going on, and ladies at tea parties were usually in rather a good mood, as Philip wisely remarked.

We rang the bell, and the drawing room door opened immediately. A young lady came out and stood looking at us for a moment before asking us what we wanted. When we held out the basket and asked her to buy some flowers, her face dimpled with amusement. I had noticed that a good many people looked amused when we told them we were flower sellers, but I never quite understood why.

"Wait a minute," she said, instead of answering our question, "I must ask my mother, and then you must come in and show us what you've picked."

She disappeared back into the drawing room, and we heard her merry laugh as she told her mother about us.

"Such a picturesque little couple, pretending to be flower sellers," we heard her say. "The boy has a face like an angel, and the girl looks like a little wild gypsy. You must see them for yourselves. I'll bring them in."

She reappeared, all smiles.

"Come in a moment," she said, "and show my mother, Mrs Sheridan, and aunt your basket. I'm sure they would like to buy some cowslips. You shall have a biscuit each, too. We're just having tea."

We trotted in after her, suspecting nothing, and then both stopped dead in the doorway, transfixed with horror.

There were four chairs placed round a little table in the window so that the ladies were sitting with their backs to us. In the first chair sat a tall, elderly lady who was evidently the mother. Next to her sat the aunt, and next to her was the empty seat which was about to be occupied by the young lady. And next to that was a high-backed armchair, with large sides, and from the depths of it came the perfectly unmistakable voice of my aunt.

"The little girl is very unruly," said the voice, confidentially. "I shall be only too glad when her mother comes and takes her off my hands."

"Run!" I whispered to Philip. "Oh, Phil, run quick!"

But Philip, in his usual slow fashion, had not yet realised what had happened. He stood there blinking as though he were in some puzzling dream. I knew he would be several minutes making up his mind to run and by that time it would be too late, so I cast about in my mind for some other way of escape.

There was one slender hope. If we walked in and stood behind my aunt's chair, it was quite impossible for her to see us without doing extraordinary gymnastics, for the chair was very big. If we were required to speak, she would certainly know it was us. However, it was our only chance. The young lady was beckoning us to come forward, wondering why we were hesitating. I took Philip's hand and led him straight to the only safe spot in the room.

Old Mrs Sheridan and her sister smiled and tried to put us at our ease. Mrs Sheridan held out her hand for a bunch of cowslips. I took two steps forward, leaned right over, thrust them at her and scuttled back to my hiding place like a frightened rabbit to its burrow. The young lady looked rather surprised, for I guessed we had not seemed shy on the doorstep, yet here we were behaving in the strangest way. Philip was standing like a stuffed image, with his mouth open, looking as though he were seeing a ghost.

"What beautiful big flowers!" said Mrs Sheridan, examining the clusters. "We shall have to go exploring and find some, too. Whereabouts did you pick these, children?"

There was dead silence. Neither of us dared speak. I heard a rustle in the armchair as though my aunt was about to turn round and examine these strange dumb specimens behind her. If her head suddenly appeared over the top of the chair I knew I should scream. So I replied, in a hoarse whisper, "In the hollow, by the stream."

"By the stream," repeated Mrs Sheridan. "Yes, I might have known these had grown near water. I shall certainly buy a bunch. Fetch my purse, Isabel, and give these two children a biscuit each before they go."

The young lady held out the plate, but to reach it we should have to walk out in the open. We shook our heads frantically, and lifted imploring eyes, but she merely thought we were being polite.

"Come along," she said, laughing, "they're very nice biscuits."

Hopelessly I took two steps forward, and leaned over as far as I could to grab two biscuits. But, as I did so, I saw my aunt's hat move, and I leaped backwards. In so doing, I bumped into a small cake stand and sent it flying, at which point my aunt's head came right round the arm of the chair, and she saw me.

I can only dimly remember what happened next. I heard my aunt say, "Philip and Ruth, what is the meaning of this?" in a voice that reminded me of a bugle blast. I heard Mrs Sheridan say, "Pick them up, Isabel! They are butter side down, all over the carpet. Don't let them get trodden in." I saw Philip move back and trip over Isabel, who was picking up buttered buns, and I noticed that her face looked as though she were trying not to laugh. I remember my aunt saying she could not understand it, a great many times, and Mrs Sheridan saying it was nothing to worry about, and we were to forget all about it.

The next thing that comes back clearly to me was my aunt's turning to us when the commotion had died down, and telling us she was taking us home to punish us most severely. But, before we went, we were to come forward and tell Mrs Sheridan how sorry we were for behaving so badly.

Philip had regained his senses by now, and he stepped forward immediately and looked up into Mrs Sheridan's face. He was truly sorry for having spoilt such a nice tea party, especially when Aunt Margaret went to so few, he said, so earnestly and politely that everyone was charmed. Even my aunt looked pleased, and if only she could have stopped there, all would have ended peacefully. But now she turned to me and asked me coldly what I had to say for myself.

I don't quite understand to this day why I was so angry, but while Philip was talking I had decided that my aunt was an idiot. There was no need to have recognised and owned us. We should never have shown we belonged to her, and then no one would have known. Therefore, I argued, she had brought all this trouble on herself, and here we were being told *we* were naughty, in front of everyone. And we weren't naughty. Why *shouldn't* we sell flowers? Anyone would think we were stealing!

All this was flashing through my rebellious little heart when my aunt spoke to me. For answer, I stuck my hands in my pockets and stamped my muddy shoes.

"I'm not a bit sorry," I stormed. "We're not doing anything wrong, and no one called us naughty till we met you. We've earned the money and it belongs to us, and we shall go on doing it if we want. You always spoil everything, Aunt Margaret."

My aunt went quite white. Never in my worst moments at home had I spoken to her like this, and here I was disgracing us all in somebody else's drawing room. I suddenly felt terrified and miserable, and ran out into the garden, leaving them all standing looking at each other.

I wanted to dash on, but realised that they might think I was running away, and I was far too proud to do that. So I walked off towards home with my hands in my pockets and my head held very high in the air. I knew my aunt and Philip were coming down the hill behind me, so I pretended to whistle. But I was too miserable to keep it up for long. When I reached home I went and stared out of the kitchen window, and tried to whistle again. I wanted to look as if nothing had happened and as though I didn't care if it had. Above all, I wasn't going to be sorry.

My aunt came in slowly, as though she was very, very tired. She crossed the room and stood beside me, looking out of the window.

"Ruth," she said, rather heavily, "I'm not going to punish you, because it doesn't seem much good. But I've been thinking it out on the way home. I don't seem able to manage you, or bring you up as I should. You have ten days' more holiday, and then, if they can take you, I am going to send you to boarding school. Your mother suggested it at Christmas, but I wanted to keep you then. Of course, it will be a big extra expense, but anything is better than have you grow up as selfish and obstinate and ill-mannered as you are now."

She turned away without looking at me, and I went on staring out of the window. I felt as though the whole world was falling down round me. I wanted to run to Philip, and bury my face in his jersey and cry as I used to when I was very tiny. But Philip had been sent straight upstairs to bed, and I was alone.

"I shan't go," I said, in what was meant to be a defiant voice, but which only sounded small and shaky.

"You won't be asked," replied my aunt, quietly.

There was a long silence, and I stood perfectly still, thinking furiously. Then I spoke again in the same small, trembling voice that tried so hard to be proud.

"All right," I announced. "I shall run away, and I shan't come back."

My aunt took no notice. I suppose she thought I often threatened to rush off like this when I was in a temper, and no doubt I would come back before dark. She sighed heavily and went slowly up to her room. And I ran out of the door.

# 7

# Running away

I did not stop for a minute when I got out to the road. I just went on running. It did not matter to me where I went so long as I got away. In my angry heart I decided that I would never, never go back again. I would be a wild little girl, or get some kind lady to adopt me, or ask someone to let me be their servant, and then perhaps Aunt Margaret would be sorry. I knew Uncle Peter would miss me when he came home every night, and of course Philip would be sad. At the thought of Philip, my eyes brimmed over, and I went on running and running with the tears streaming down my cheeks, quite breathless, and sobbing.

"I am going to send you to boarding school." I kept whispering the horrible words to myself, and trying to take it all in. I saw myself going away in disgrace, alone in a train to a building which I imagined would be rather like Worcester jail. And I imagined Terry and Philip sitting in the wigwam together, with the birds singing and the foxgloves sprouting up above the bracken and the wild roses uncurling in the hedges. And I should not be there. Then other pictures seemed to dance before my eyes: Philip kneeling alone at the bedroom window with the sun rising over the Ankerdines, and my little bed empty. Philip lying on his tummy in the hayfields, writing his book, and I should not be there to draw the pictures.

It was quiet all round me as I rushed along. I had met no one and, except for the cries of birds going to bed and my own sobbing, the world had seemed quite silent. But now I suddenly became aware of the sound of children's voices and the barking of a dog, so I rubbed away the tears with the back of my hand and looked about me.

I had reached the entrance to a village where I had been once or twice before. It was a very small village: only a few cottages, a white square school, a village shop, and a church. It nestled in a dip of the low hills just where the country road met a larger main road with a signpost pointing to Bromyard.

I stood for some little time wondering what to do. I did not want to walk through the village just yet, for I knew that everyone would think I had been crying. Besides, I was hot and tired, and my head was beginning to ache. I wanted to sit somewhere cool and quiet, where I could rest, and think where to go next. I looked all round me, and then realised that I was standing by a little brown wooden gate that led into the churchyard, and the church door was open. I thought no one was likely to go into church as late as this and, even if they did, I could crouch down in a pew, and they would not see me. So I went up the path between the rows of quiet gravestones, reading the names as I went past.

One stone interested me especially, and I stopped to read it again. It was a little white cross, marking a garden of forget-me-nots. On it was written: "Jane Collins, aged 9 years. Went to be with the Lord, April 5th, 1900."

I read it several times, and then shivered at the thought of poor little Jane Collins who had had to leave this world on an April day with its sunshine and its lambs, its singing birds and first flowers. Death had always seemed a distant thing, to be thought about by old people and clergymen. But Jane Collins was only 9 years old when she went to be with the Lord. What if I, aged 9, had suddenly to go and be with the Lord? What would he say to me about all my tempers, and the lies I'd told, and the times I'd run away instead of helping, and the dust under the carpet? It would be far, far worse than going to boarding school. For the first time in my life I began to feel really frightened about being so naughty.

I walked on into the church porch, and peeped cautiously inside. It was quite empty, so I slipped through the door and began wandering round, looking at the inscriptions, and the pictures, and the daffodils in vases. One thing pleased me most of all. That was the evening light streaming through the stained glass windows and falling in coloured patterns on the stone floor, making a sort of fairy track all up the western side of the church.

As I stood watching, it suddenly came over me how terribly tired I was. The church was so quiet and cool and friendly, with its sunset light and its daffodils, that I thought I would lie down and rest a little before deciding what to do next. So I collected some footstools, made a little mattress, wrapped myself up in an old black cassock that hung near the door, and cuddled down inside one of the pews where I could watch the beautiful patterns and think things out.

But I had not realised how sleepy I really was. I had been out in the open air all day, I had been very frightened and very angry and very miserable. I had run nearly three miles on a warm spring evening. In fact, I was so tired that I hardly remember laying my head down on the footstool. But just as I was dropping off, I thought I saw Jane Collins standing in the sunset light of the west window, pointing upwards along the golden rays. She was a little girl just like me, with dark plaits and a pinafore and blue socks.

The moment I saw her face, I knew I had made a mistake in pitying her, for never before, either in dreams or real life, had I seen a child look so radiantly happy. Her arms were full of Easter flowers, and somehow I knew perfectly well that they would never fade or die. Then the light grew dim and blurred and I fell into a deep, deep sleep.

When I woke up I was lying in the dark, and for a long time I could not imagine where I was. I was very stiff, and cold, and sore, for the footstools had come apart and I was lying partly on the stone floor.

I sat up. As soon as I lifted my face, I found that a wonderful thing had happened. The day was beginning to dawn, and a grey light was stealing through the eastern windows on the other side of the church. The darkness had scattered, and with it all my terrors and nightmares. I gave a great sigh of relief, and sat quite still with my small face turned towards the morning.

And as I sat there waiting and listening, the silence was broken by the clear call of one bird, and I realised with a thrill of joy that the world was waking up again after the terrible night. Then another bird woke and answered, then another, until it seemed as though every bird in the county must be singing itself hoarse. And, as I sat listening, the grey light gave place to gold, and the whole bird choir seemed to go crazy with joy. The sun was rising, and morning had come again.

The relief was so great that I did not want to move. I forgot that I was cold and hungry and only remembered that the night was over, and that I was no longer alone, because the birds had woken up. Soon I would slip out of the church and run home to Philip, but for the moment I was content to sit and listen.

But I did not sit and listen for long, for somehow my head fell over on to the footstools and I fell fast asleep again. When I woke the next time it was very suddenly, for the church was flooded with light, and there were heavy footsteps coming up the aisle.

I lay quite still and waited as the footsteps came nearer, and then my curiosity got the better of me. I crawled to the end of the pew and peeped into the aisle. It was a clergyman. He was walking slowly up the church, looking up at the eastern windows. He need not have seen me at all, for his head was turned away and I was quite small enough to creep under the seat. I was just about to do this, for I did not want to be seen. Children were not allowed to sleep in churches, I was sure, and there was a county police station just down the road. But I had been lying all night in a draughty church with my legs on a stone floor, and I had caught a cold, so I was only half out of sight when a dreadful thing happened.

I sneezed!

I tried to stop, but it was no use. Out it came with a loud explosion, and the clergyman jumped. Then he came and looked over the side of the pew. There, of course, he saw half a little girl, wrapped up in a cassock, sticking out from under the seat.

He said nothing, but came inside and sat down. Then he leaned over and spoke very gently.

"Come out," he said. "There's no need to hide under the seat. I don't mind children in my church."

I uncurled slowly, sat down on the seat beside him, and looked up into his face. He was not very young and not very old, and his eyes were blue and kind. He reminded me of the old shepherd, somehow, only he was not wrinkled and whiskery. It was just that he was the sort of man I was not afraid of talking to.

"I couldn't help being here," I explained. "I came in last night when the door was open, and I went to sleep by mistake. I put on your clothes because I was cold, but I didn't mean to stay all night. Only when I woke up the first time it was too dark to move, and when I woke up the second time it was morning."

He looked rather startled. "Do you mean that you have been here all night?" he asked. "Whatever is your mother thinking? We must let her know where you are at once."

I was silent a moment, twisting my hands together. I had a sudden funny feeling that I wanted to tell someone all about it, and I thought this man would do.

"It's not my mother," I whispered, "it's my aunt. I wouldn't have done it with my mother. I've been very, very naughty, and my aunt's going to send me away to boarding school because she can't manage me. I didn't want to go, so I ran away, and here I am."

I looked up to see if he was very shocked, but he didn't seem to be. He just looked very interested and rather sorry for me.

"I'm glad you told me that," he said gravely, "and I should like you to tell me a great deal more about it. But first of all we must tell your aunt where you are. Then, perhaps, when she knows you're safe, she will let you stay a little, and we can talk. Are you on the phone?"

We were, and I knew the number.

"Good," said my friend. "We'll go straight back to the vicarage, ring up your aunt, and tell her all about it. What's your name? I'm Mr Robinson."

We walked out of the church together. The world was radiant with song and light and colour, but I knew it must be very early morning, because the flower petals were still closed.

"Why did you come to church so early?" I asked suddenly.

"I came to say my prayers," answered the clergyman. "I often come out early, because everything looks so beautiful. Don't you think that these buttercups are enough to make anyone feel good and happy?"

I looked at the buttercups, but I did not feel happy, and I was quite certain I should never be good. I didn't know how to, and I said so.

"But don't you want to be good?" he asked.

I wrinkled my brow. "Ye-es, sometimes. But even if I was to really try to be good, I'm sure I could never manage it. I keep being naughty."

And my new friend nodded, and smiled.

# 8

# I make a new friend

We went into the vicarage and the clergyman took me straight to his study. It was a big sunny room, full of books and, while I sat and rested in a big armchair, he went away to telephone. He was gone a long time. Having nothing else to do, I got up and began to wander round the room looking at the pictures. They were mostly photographs and not very interesting, but there was one that I liked so much that I moved my chair over in front of it so that I could sit and gaze at it.

It was the picture of a sheep lost on a rocky mountainside. Overhead hovered a fierce bird, waiting for it to die, and the sheep was looking up and crying to be rescued. I could see that someone had heard its cry, for the shepherd with his crook was leaning over the precipice. In another moment he would pick it up and carry it safe home in his arms.

I was so intent on the picture that I never noticed that the clergyman had come back. Now he stood in front of me with a tray which he laid down beside me.

"I've telephoned your aunt," he said. "She's been very anxious about you, and the police and your uncle have been out looking for you all night. However, now she knows you're safe, she doesn't mind you staying to breakfast with me. Afterwards, you must run home and tell her how sorry you are."

I fell upon the tray of food with a tremendous appetite. It was such a nice breakfast, too, with a boiled egg and strawberry jam and a teapot all to myself. I munched away most contentedly. Mr Robinson sat down on the sofa while I ate my breakfast, and we talked. I told him all about Philip and Terry, and Philip's book, and the wigwam, and the camera, and the flower selling. He asked a great many questions, and seemed really interested in it all.

But when I had finished my last mouthful of bread and jam, I realised that now I should probably be sent straight home. I didn't want to go just yet for I thought my new friend was one of the nicest men I had ever met, except perhaps for Mr Tandy the old shepherd. So I laid down my tray and pointed at the picture on the wall.

"Isn't that a nice picture?" I remarked. "It reminds me of the shepherd at home. One of his lambs escaped, like the one in the picture, and he went to look for it. I went, too. We looked for ever so long, and then we found it all tangled up in a thorn bush, crying, and it took Mr Tandy ages to get it out. His hands got all torn and scratched to bits in the thorns. But the lamb was all right, though."

My friend was looking at the picture, also. He did not answer for a minute.

"Ruth," he said suddenly, "how did the lamb get into such a place? Why did he ever get lost?"

"Well," I replied, "I suppose he ran away. They often do."

"Yes," went on the clergyman – and he was speaking very earnestly now. "But why did he run away? He had a kind shepherd and a very nice green field. Why didn't he stay there?"

"Well," I answered thoughtfully, "I expect he thought it looked nicer beyond his field, and went to see. Then I expect he got lost, and when he wanted to go back he just couldn't find the way."

"You're quite right," said Mr Robinson. "Just look at the sheep in the picture. I expect he had been trying to find his way back all night. But he was lost, and the further he went, the steeper the rocks became, and the more hopeless he felt. So I think he stopped trying at last, and just stood quite still at the edge of the precipice. And what did he do then, Ruth?"

I looked up at him. I was beginning to understand that he was not talking about a real sheep any longer.

"I don't know," I whispered, rather shyly.

"Well, then, I'll tell you," went on my friend. "I think he looked round and saw a precipice underneath him, and big rocks above him, and he said to himself, 'It's no good. I can't possibly get back by myself. There's only one person who can take me home, and that's the shepherd.' So he opened his mouth and gave a little cry. The shepherd had been waiting all night for that little cry. As soon as he heard it, he leaned over and picked up the sheep, and carried it safely back to his own pasture. And I don't know who was the happier, the sheep or the shepherd."

My eyes were fixed on him. I knew now that he was talking about me.

"I ran away, too, and got lost last night, didn't I?" I whispered again.

"You did," answered Mr Robinson, "and, do you know, when I found you hiding in the church and you told me that you'd run away and then you said you didn't know how to be good, I thought to myself, 'Here's one of

God's lost lambs trying to get back by herself.' You'll never do it, Ruth. There's only one Person who can take you back into God's way and keep you there, and that is the Lord Jesus Christ, who called himself the Good Shepherd."

"Then why doesn't he do it?" I asked.

"Because you are still trying to get back without him," came the answer. "You may want to be good, but you keep being naughty instead. Well, every time you are naughty you are getting a little bit further away from God's way, and a little bit more lost than you were before."

"What if I *really* tried to be good?" I said frowning. "I mean, if I really tried hard?"

"No, Ruth. It's no use. You can't make yourself good, and if we've ever done that, we've got to stop trying. You've got to tell the Shepherd that you are quite lost, and ask him to find you and take you back into God's way, and to make you one of his own obedient lambs."

"Will he really do it?" I asked.

"Ruth," said Mr Robinson suddenly, "how old are you?"

"Nine," I answered, wondering what that had to do with it.

"Well then, he's been loving you and looking for you for nine whole years. Don't you think he'll be glad to hear you call to him, when he's been waiting for such a long time?"

I sat very still, thinking hard.

"Is it really all I've got to do to be good?" I asked at last. "I thought it was very difficult to be good."

"It's all you must do at first," he answered. "That's the wonderful part. You see, the Good Shepherd has done it all for you. He took away sin – all our wrongdoings – when he died for us on the cross. That means we can be forgiven without any punishment. When we ask him to forgive us, he does, straight away. You told me that your friend's hands got torn and scratched as he rescued that lamb. But he lifted the lamb out of the thorns without hurting it at all. And in just the same way, the Good Shepherd was wounded and hurt when he came to look for you. He has done everything, and all you've to do is to say 'Thank you', and believe that his wounded hands can lift you up and carry you back to God's fold as soon as you ask him."

"And what happens then?" I asked. "Shall I always be good after that?"

He smiled.

"You won't always be good all at once," he replied, "but you will always belong to the Good Shepherd, and he will begin to teach you how to be good. He will often speak to you in your heart, and you must learn to listen to his voice. When he speaks, you must always obey. And you must learn to talk to him about everything, too. We call it praying, but really it means sharing everything with the Shepherd."

Once more we sat still for a long time. At last Mr Robinson spoke.

"I have to go to my church now," he said gently, "and you must go home, or your aunt will think you've run away somewhere else. But before you go, I'm going to give you a copy of that picture for your very own. Take it with you and look at it often. Each time you look at it, remember that you are that lost lamb and that the Good Shepherd is waiting to find you as soon as you ask him. One other thing – have you a Bible of your own?"

I said I had a very nice Bible in my drawer at home.

"Then when you get home find the Gospel of Luke, and read a little bit every night. It will tell you all the story of the Shepherd and how he came to earth to look for lost sheep. And when you've finished it, read the other Gospels."

He had opened a drawer and produced a postcard-size copy of the picture on the wall. I took it, and whispered my thanks.

I followed him out, holding my new treasure tightly in both hands. He came to the front gate and stood watching me as I set out along the road. When I had gone about a little way, I turned round and ran back. I stood on tiptoe and he put his head down so that I could whisper in his ear.

"Shall I come back and tell you when it's happened?" I asked.

He nodded. "I was hoping you would," he admitted. "I shall always be glad to see you, so come whenever you like."

So I left him and turned the corner. The road ahead of me led back home, and at the thought of home my heart beat rather fast. What would my aunt and uncle say to me, and what should I say to them?

But I did not worry much, for I had more important things to think about. I would find some quiet place far away from everyone, and before I went back home I would ask the Good Shepherd to find me and make me one of his lambs.

I was very choosy about the spot. The fields would not do, because I could be seen from the road, and I wanted to be quite alone. So I trotted on until I came to that part where the road ran between woods and I remembered that the boughs nearly met overhead. Here I climbed the bank and slipped in and out among the trees till I had reached a little clearing right away from any path. Here the moss grew thick on the ground and clematis hung in curtains round me. Here I knelt down among the primroses and felt as though I were in some secret chapel, far away from the world.

I looked again at my picture, but at first I dared not pray. I felt as if my whole life was going to depend on the next few moments. What if I spoke and nothing happened? What if the Shepherd had gone away and was not listening any more?

Then I spoke aloud to the Good Shepherd. I told him about my naughtiness, and how I couldn't be good by myself. I told him I was sorry because I'd kept him waiting so long. Then I asked him to forgive me and find me and pick me up in his arms, and never to let me run away from him again.

Then I waited, perfectly still, for my answer, almost expecting to feel the gentle arms thrown round me. And what happened? I heard nothing, and I felt nothing, but I knew that my prayer was heard. I could not possibly have put it into words, but I knew that love and forgiveness were round about me as certainly as the sunlight and the quiet air. I knew at that instant that I was sought and loved and found.

I was so happy that I stayed where I was for a long time, as though by moving I might ruin the beautiful peace of those moments. I was not only happy, I was grateful, too. I remembered how long Jesus, the Good Shepherd, had waited. I thought of Mr Tandy's poor bleeding hands, and remembered how the hands of the Shepherd had been wounded when he died on the cross for me. I did not understand it all, but the clergyman had said that the Bible made it very plain, and I believed him. So I folded my hands again and tried to thank him.

Then it suddenly struck me that I was supposed to be going home. My aunt was waiting for me. So I left my little sanctuary, and went back to the road.

But I walked very slowly. Would she be very angry with me? I wondered. And, worst of all, would I be naughty and rude again? My rudeness seemed to come out whether I wanted it to or not, and if I was naughty now everything would be spoilt.

Then I remembered something else. The Shepherd had picked me up in his arms, and I could tell him everything if he was really as close to me as all that. So I told him all about it as I trotted home, and somehow all my happiness came back to me. I was not alone any longer.

I swallowed hard as I opened the front door and slipped inside – a dirty, scared, untidy little figure clasping my hands tightly together in the hall. I had no idea what I was going to say to my aunt. Only to myself I kept whispering the words, "Even if I'm punished, help me to be good."

Then my aunt suddenly appeared at the kitchen door, and we both stood looking at each other in silence.

But the loving Shepherd had found me, and I found out that when we first come to know his love, he begins to make us more loving, too. As I stood stiffly in the hall, something happened to my hard little heart that I had not expected. I suddenly ran forward and flung myself into my aunt's arms.

"I'm sorry, Auntie," I whispered. "I want to be good. And please, please, don't send me to boarding school. I want to stay with you here, and I'll never, never run away or be naughty again."

My aunt, kneeling in the passage, pressed my tear-stained cheek against hers and held me close to her. Then she smoothed back my tangled hair and kissed me.

"Ruth," she whispered back, "I don't want to send you away if I can possibly help it. We'll try again."

Then she took my hand and led me to the table in the kitchen, where I sat down and ate a whole second breakfast to make up for my lack of supper the night before.

# 9

# My sheep know my voice

I caught a bad cold from sleeping in the church, and had to go to bed for three days. Philip stayed with me most of the time, so we put in a lot of work on the bird book. When we were tired of drawing and writing we lay and talked. He was never tired of hearing about my night in the church, and I was enormously flattered to hear how much everybody had missed me.

"I don't think Auntie or Uncle went to bed all night," Philip informed me. "I couldn't go to sleep either. I thought you might be dead, and I was crying and crying in bed. Then I went downstairs and I found Auntie crying a little bit in the kitchen. We had a lovely drink of cocoa together, and she gave me a chocolate biscuit, and we sat by the fire and talked."

I felt rather hurt that Philip should have found such comfort in a chocolate biscuit when I might have been lying dead in a ditch.

"What did you talk about?" I said, hoping it had been about me.

"Oh, lots of things," answered my brother cheerfully. "I said perhaps you'd been drowned in Whippet brook. Auntie said she thought you were probably just hiding, and she might send you to boarding school as a punishment. I said I thought that was a bad idea."

"Why?" I said hopefully.

"Because I shouldn't have anyone to play with outside school," he explained. "I said I thought it wouldn't be any use, because you would run away at once."

"What did she say, then?"

"She said you wouldn't be able to. So I said it would be a pity to send you to boarding school, in any case, because I should probably have a nervous breakdown."

"Whatever's that?" I asked, with great interest.

"Oh, it's an illness you get when people do things you don't like. I heard Auntie talking about someone who had a nervous breakdown because the cook went away. So I said I would have one if you went away."

"Is it like measles?" I asked. Measles was the only illness I had ever had, and I thought it of great importance.

"Oh, I don't know," answered Philip. "I don't think it's got spots. But it doesn't matter, anyhow. You're not going now. But you'll have to be very careful about being good, because once she's thought of it she may think of it again."

I was silent. I hadn't told anyone yet about what had happened to me in the wood, for somehow I did not know how to put it into words. How could I persuade Philip that something had really taken place? There was nothing to show for it. Sometimes, lying there with a sore throat and a stopped-up nose, I began to wonder how much of it was true, or whether perhaps I'd imagined it. Then I would take out my precious picture and look at it until my doubts disappeared. I would bury my face in the pillow and ask the Shepherd to let me feel close to him again.

There was my Bible, too. As soon as I got home, I found it in the drawer and started to read it. After much searching I found the chapter Mr Tandy had read to me about the sheep that was lost. I read it over to myself again and again until I almost knew it by heart. I read the rest of the chapter, too, about the boy who ran away, just like me, and who came home again and said he was sorry, and was forgiven by his father. I thought it was exactly like me and Aunt Margaret. I liked it very much indeed.

I tried to pray, too. I had been taught to say my prayers, but somehow it was different now. Before, it was just saying words because I thought I ought to, but now I was talking to Someone I knew and who loved me.

It was on my second night in bed that I made a great discovery. Philip had gone down to supper, and I had pulled out my Bible from under my pillow, for I was rather shy of letting anyone see me read it. As I turned the pages of the Gospels, looking for stories, I came across John chapter 10, and the word "Shepherd" caught my eye at once.

I had often heard the chapter read in church and at school, but I had forgotten where in the Bible it came. Now I read it eagerly, for it was the very thing I was hungering for. Here it was, all over again: "I am the good shepherd, and the good shepherd gives up his life for his sheep." I knew that meant that the Shepherd had to come to die on the cross before he could find me.

I did not understand the verses about thieves and robbers, but I understood about the sheep following. That meant being good and doing what the Shepherd said. But what could it mean about "The sheep know their shepherd's voice"? The clergyman had said that Jesus would speak to me, and that I must obey. But although I had lain in bed with my eyes shut, listening hard, I could hear nothing. The room seemed perfectly silent, and I did so want the Good Shepherd to say something to me. How could I know his voice if he never spoke to me?

This question troubled me quite a lot that night and next day, until I suddenly had a good idea. I would go and see Mr Tandy, take him my postcard and tell him all about what had happened. Perhaps he would be able to tell me about the Shepherd's voice.

I was very impatient to get up after this, and was allowed to go down to tea on the fourth day. At last, on the fifth day, which to my relief was sunny, I was able to go to the woods again, with Philip. It seemed a special afternoon, with the end of the holidays so near. I could have stayed there for ever. But suddenly I thought of something.

"Philip," I said, "I'm going home now. You see, I specially want to visit somebody on the way back."

"All right," answered Philip. "We'll go. Who do you want to visit?"

"Mr Tandy, the shepherd," I replied.

"Good!" agreed Philip. "I like Mr Tandy. I'll come with you."

I stopped dead, wondering how I could explain. Philip walked on, watching a magpie, unaware of any difficulty.

"Philip," I said, rather awkwardly, "you can't come with me. You see, it's a secret, and I want to see Mr Tandy alone. It's something you don't know about, and I've got to go by myself."

It was Philip's turn to stop and stare now. He turned right round and looked as though he thought he had heard wrongly.

"But why?" he asked at last. "You always tell me your secrets. You shouldn't tell Mr Tandy before me. I'm your brother, and he's only an old man."

There was a sort of shadow in his clear blue eyes, and his face was rather red. I could see he was hurt, and I felt dreadful.

"But you wouldn't understand," I explained desperately. "You see, it's not a make-up or a pretend. It's a real, true, very important secret. You might not believe me and you might laugh."

He looked not only hurt, but downright indignant.

"But I've never laughed before," he said, rather pitifully, "and I always believe you. You're unkind, Ruth, to have real true secrets and not tell me. I always tell you mine."

There was a long pause, and I did not know what to say.

"Oh, all right," he said at last, trying to speak casually. "I'll go on home. You'll find me in the orchard when you come."

He turned and went on, and I followed rather miserably. We walked single file in silence as far as the stile where the path divided. One way led over the meadow towards home and one led up to the sheepfolds.

"Goodbye," said Philip without looking round. "See you later."

He took the downward path and I took the upward one, but I had not gone many steps before I turned to look back. Philip was walking slowly across the meadow with his hands in his pockets and his head rather bowed as though he were staring hard at the ground. He must have been very miserable indeed, for he was not even watching the sky for birds.

And as I stood staring after his lonely little figure, I saw all in a flash – perhaps for the first time – what sort of a brother Philip had been to me. I remembered how gravely he had listened when I used to snuggle my curly head against his shoulder and whisper my baby ideas into his ear. How patiently he had entered into my make-believes with my dolls. How swiftly he would run back from school in case I should be missing him. And how faithfully he had stood by me when I was cross and bad-tempered and punished! As I thought of all these things, I suddenly didn't want to have any secret at all that I could not share with Philip. Of course, I wanted to go on belonging to the Good Shepherd, but not by myself. Philip must belong, too, and then we could enjoy the secret together.

I flew down the hill after him as fast as my legs would carry me, shouting his name at the top of my voice. He turned round and waited for me and, even as I ran, I could not help thinking how much nicer he was than me. I should have walked on in a huff and pretended not to hear.

I was quite breathless when I reached him, and sort of fell against him to stop myself.

"Philip," I gasped. "I didn't mean it at all. I don't want to have secrets without you, and I'll tell you everything always. Only, you see, there's a bit I don't understand and I can't tell you properly until I've asked Mr Tandy. But then I shall know all about it and I'll tell you in the wigwam tomorrow and then you can have it, too."

The shadow passed instantly from Philip's eyes, and his beautiful smile shone out again. There never was a boy so quick to forgive and forget a quarrel.

"It's all right," he assured me. "I don't mind you going to tell Mr Tandy, as long as you tell me afterwards. But it will spoil everything if we don't tell each other *all* our secrets."

I was so pleased to see him happy again that I flung my arms round his neck and kissed him. I had not done such a thing for a long time, and he looked a little breathless and astonished, and glanced round the field to see that no one was looking. Then he gave me another radiant smile, and trotted off towards home.

I turned and ran back up the hill, but when I had gone halfway up I turned to look at Philip. He was still trotting, but his head was thrown far back. He had forgotten all about everything and was watching swifts.

I felt very hot in the face when I reached the sheepfolds, because I had climbed the hill so fast. To my great relief Mr Tandy was there mending the gate, and I ran straight up to him.

"Mr Tandy," I said, without waiting for any introductions, "I've come to tell you something. I've found out all about that story you read me, and I know now that it means me, and that the Good Shepherd is Jesus."

He stood there with his hammer in his hand, looking down at me, with a look of the most amazing joy on his face.

"I'm real glad to hear it, little maid," he said, rather huskily. "Maybe you'll tell me a bit more about it."

"Oh, yes," I replied. I told him everything – about running away, and Mr Robinson and the picture and me belonging to the Shepherd.

Mr Tandy listened gravely, but his wrinkled old face was alight with happiness.

"Thank God for that, little maid!" he replied, "for if you belong to him now, you'll belong to him for ever. No one can snatch you out of his hand."

"Mr Tandy," I asked, "are you one of his sheep?"

"Sure, little maid," he answered, "I've been one of his flock for nearly fifty years."

"Then, Mr Tandy," I went on eagerly, "have you ever heard his voice? It says his sheep know his voice. But I've listened and listened, and he never says anything to me, and I do want to hear him so badly."

He thought a long time before answering that question. Then he spoke very slowly.

"I'm going to call my sheep, lassie," he said. "And when I call, take a look at 'em all. But you specially mark them ones over by the hedge, and see the difference."

I watched, fascinated, while he gave a low, clear call. Every sheep in the meadow lifted its head expectantly and drew a step or two nearer, except for the group by the hedge. They went on feeding quietly as though nothing had happened.

"Why don't they answer?" I asked. "Can't they hear you?"

"They hears me well enough," answered the old man, "but they don't know my voice from all the others because they belonged to another shepherd who was took sick. They only joined my flock two days gone. But let 'em walk to the pastures with me for a week or so, and let me fold 'em, and put my hands on their heads, and feed 'em, and they'll soon come to know my voice same as the rest. Now there's a-many voices speaking to your heart, little maid, and you've only belonged to the Shepherd these few days. So maybe you haven't learned to pick out his voice from all them others – for 'tis only a little, quiet voice."

"Then tell me how I can start," I pleaded.

"Well, 'tis like this," he said at last, after another long pause. "Do you ever want to be a bad little lass?"

"Oh yes, often," I replied. "Before I ran away, I used to lose my temper and be rude to Aunt Margaret nearly every day."

"Well then," went on Mr Tandy, "you mind this: next time you want to lose your temper, you remember there's mainly two voices a-speaking to you. There's the voice of the enemy – that is, the devil, what don't want you to listen to the Shepherd. He'll be telling you to kick up a row and stamp your foot and all the rest of it. But if you hold back a minute and listen, maybe you'll hear another voice... a little quiet-like voice, telling you be gentle and do as you're told. That's the voice of the Shepherd. And if you learn to mind that voice, he'll speak again, and you'll find you're hearing him all the time and everywhere. He talks to me out in these fields, and when I reads my Bible he comes to me. And I know it ain't just a book of black and white print for scholars, but 'tis the voice of my Saviour a-speaking to me."

Drawn by his gentle voice, the sheep had come quite close and were standing near his knees, their mild faces upturned. When he stopped speaking they moved away, cropping the grass.

"'Twill soon be time for the shearing," observed the old man thoughtfully.

"Thank you very much, Mr Tandy," I said. "I'm going home now to listen, and I hope I shall soon want to get into a temper just so I can hear Jesus' voice."

He shook his head. "Don't you hope for any such thing!" he warned me. "And don't you try it alone.

Remember, it is only the Saviour who can stop you from doing wrong."

He spoke very earnestly, and I thought about it a lot as I ran home across the fields. How strange it was that I couldn't ever stop myself from losing my own temper! Yet I knew I couldn't, because I'd tried. Not very often, it was true, but I *had* tried at least once or twice.

Philip was not in the orchard, so I went to look for him indoors. Rather to my dismay, I heard voices in the dining room. They had started tea, and I was late. We were not allowed to be late for tea, so I stepped into the room rather guiltily, with an anxious glance at Aunt Margaret. She was looking extremely grim.

"Ruth," she said sharply, "you're late again and I'm not going to have it. Sit down and eat your tea in silence. And you are not to have a chocolate biscuit."

Now this was a dreadful punishment, because I loved chocolate biscuits, and we hardly ever had them. I gave a little stamp with my foot and threw back my head. All my happiness disappeared and a great torrent of angry words seemed to come springing up out of my heart all ready to tumble out of my mouth. In fact, I had actually opened my mouth, when I suddenly remembered!

If I got in a rage now I shouldn't be able to listen to the little quiet voice of the Good Shepherd. And, if I didn't listen now, perhaps he wouldn't speak to me again!

It was so difficult to stop those angry words that I had to clap my hand in front of my mouth to keep them in. And so I stood in the middle of the room, listening, while my aunt and Philip stared at me in the greatest astonishment.

"What is the matter?" asked my aunt, coldly. "Have you bitten your tongue?"

I didn't answer, because it had suddenly come back to me – the verse that Mr Tandy and I had been talking about: "The sheep know their shepherd's voice. He calls each of them by name and... they follow, because they know his voice." Following the Shepherd meant being like him. If I was going to be like him, I must stop stamping, shouting, answering back and sulking, because I knew the Lord Jesus had never done any of these things. "Help me to follow you," I whispered in my heart. "Stop me being angry, quick!"

I drew a great big breath and put my hand back in my pocket. Then I sat down in my chair without saying anything, for my anger was all going away. Aunt Margaret still continued to stare at me, as though she was rather scared as to what might happen next. But I went on munching my bread and butter in silence. I did not look at the chocolate biscuits, because I was afraid the sight of them might make me angry again.

We were all very quiet for the rest of tea, and when it was finished, Aunt Margaret said that as it was my first day up after my cold, I had better go straight to bed. I did not mind at all, for I had such a lot to think about that I wanted to be alone. I got in bed, and lay by my open window staring out at the summer dusk.

The sky was the colour of deep harebells, and when I'd stared at it a long time I suddenly discovered that there were stars hidden in its blue depths. I lay with my arms thrown above my head on the pillow, looking and listening, till I fell asleep. I was perfectly happy, because for the very first time, I had heard the voice of the Good Shepherd.

# 10

# The accident

We meant to go straight to the wigwam next day, and talk about the secret. But just as we climbed over the stile, Terry popped up out of the ditch like a rabbit and said he'd come to spend the morning with us. He had hidden in the ditch to give us a surprise. So, having been duly surprised, we all settled down on the bank to make plans.

As a matter of fact Terry had already made all the plans, and we were merely meant to follow them. He had found a high ash tree with a wood pigeon's nest at the top and if Philip wanted to see a wood pigeon's egg, he'd better come along right now because there were two beauties. It was an ash tree with a fork. Terry's plan was to collect some branches and bits of wood and make a sort of platform where we could sit and watch the eggs hatch.

We were thrilled with the idea, and went scuttling off single file through the woods. The tree in question was quite a long way away, across the stream in the valley, and some way in among the larches that grew on the further side. The larches were beautiful by now, studded all over with crimson baby cones, like jewels on a coronet, the sweeping boughs such a vivid green that other trees looked dull in comparison. When I was tiny I always imagined that the fairies swung on the larch boughs, but now I knew better. Yet I still loved them and I lingered behind for a moment to finger the tassels while the boys went crashing on ahead. The tree was well off the beaten track, and the brambles and nettles grew thick around here. I followed in their path as best I could but, even so, my bare legs got dreadfully scratched, and were the colour of unripe blackberries when I finally caught up. I sat down on the tree root and began mopping up the scratches with my handkerchief.

"Sorry," said Philip, apologetically. "I forgot your legs were shorter than ours for jumping. You keep up on the way home and I'll tread the brambles down for you."

Terry stared at my damaged knees. "She's a game little kid, ain't she?" he observed, and I felt myself glowing with his praise. I would willingly have walked through brambles and nettles to have earned such praise.

Terry had no time to waste. He crouched like a small panther and then leaped for the nearest bough of the ash. He caught hold with one hand and dragged himself up, the muscles rippling all over his taut little body.

"Now," he yelled, lying astride the bough, "hoist up Ruth, and I'll catch hold!"

Philip heaved me up on his shoulders and Terry seized my wrists and pulled until I was able to clutch the bough. I gave a convulsive wriggle, more or less turned myself inside out, and arrived panting beside Terry. Philip gave two mighty leaps, but fell backwards. On the third he caught hold of the branch and dragged himself up too. So we sat dangling our legs, and we shared our elevenses with Terry. He always took it for granted that my aunt included him when she prepared our food, and always ate much more than his share. But we gave it ungrudgingly, for we had long ago decided that Terry's mother must starve him at home, as no one but a starving child could eat so wolfishly.

"Come on," said Terry, gulping down the last mouthful, "we'll nip up and take a look at her."

Off he went like a sailor on a rope, while Philip and I followed more slowly. The nest was on a sort of platform of interwoven twigs, and as we got nearer to it we could hear the nervous murmur of the pigeon deep in her throat. Then suddenly there was a whirr of beautiful pearl-grey wings and the bird rose and settled on the very topmost twig of the opposite fork, where she sat looking down at us and her nest.

It was such a careless nest that I wondered how it was that the eggs escaped rolling out. It was just a few loosely woven sticks with some moss stuffed in the holes. But the eggs were burning hot and well cared for, and the mother was in a frenzy of anxiety. Terry leaned back and stared at her.

"Nice spot to watch them eggs from," he remarked coolly. "I'm a-going up there myself."

"You couldn't!" protested Philip. "The branches wouldn't hold you. They'll hardly hold the pigeon."

But Terry was rather a boastful boy. If anyone ever said "you couldn't do" a thing, he immediately had to do it to show that he could. So now he merely said, "Garn, I'll show you," and swung himself across to the opposite fork.

Philip and I watched in fascinated silence, as the agile little figure mounted higher and higher. The pigeon saw him coming, rose softly, and alighted back with half-spread wings on to her nest. We both stared at Terry. We had seen him do daring and almost impossible feats before, but this beat all. Already the grey stems were bending outwards beneath his weight.

"Stop!" called Philip in a rather husky voice. But Terry took no notice. Instead, his happy laugh came ringing back to us through the leaves, and still he climbed – only he was climbing very cautiously now.

"He's got there!" breathed Philip, and indeed he had. He was standing out right against the sky, clinging to a frail branch. The wind that moved lazily over the tree tops had caught his hair and blown it back from his face, and his dark starry eyes were bright with laughter and triumph.

As we watched, Terry, ignoring our frightened pleadings, began to swing to and fro. Twice the branch bowed with him, but the third time it snapped. Terry was flung outward into space.

He gave one shrill scream that shattered the silence of the woods, and haunted me in the night for many weeks to come. Then we heard his light body crashing through the leaves and twigs, which mercifully partly broke his fall. Then came a sickening thud… and then silence.

I don't know to this day how Philip and I escaped falling after him and breaking our necks, we swung down that tree at such a speed. Even so, Philip reached the bottom long before I did. But I got there somehow, and dropped on to the ground gasping and sobbing, and lay in a trembling heap with my face hidden in the moss. I dared not look at Terry.

But Philip was down on his knees beside him, and had come to the conclusion that Terry was still breathing. He came over to me at last and put his arm around me.

"Ruth," he said, in a voice that was shaky and fearful, "I'm not quite sure, but I think he's alive. We can't possibly carry him. We shall have to fetch some men and a doctor. I think I'd better go, because I can run faster than you and I'm not crying so much. But, Ruth, we can't leave him alone, because he might wake up and be frightened and want someone. So would you mind staying with him, and I'll come back as quick as I can?"

I shuddered and shook my head violently. I couldn't be left alone – I was much too frightened. I clung to him, sobbing, and begged him to let me go instead. But Philip wouldn't hear of it.

"You see, Ruth," he explained urgently, "he may die, and if the doctor came in time he may be able to do something to make him better. I shall get there much quicker because of my legs being so much longer. You must let me go at once, and try to be brave and stop crying."

He freed himself from my grasp, gently enough, and made off like the wind. I lay and listened to his footsteps crackling over the dead leaves and twigs, until the sound died away and only the murmuring of the pigeons broke the silence of the woods.

Now that I was left alone, it occurred to me that I must make myself look at Terry. So I clenched my teeth and my fists, and sat up.

What I actually saw was a great relief to me. I had never seen anyone badly hurt or unconscious before, and I had imagined that it would be a very scary sight. But Terry, lying on his back with his arms spread wide, might have been asleep, except that his lips were unnaturally pale, and he breathed so lightly. He did not look hurt or frightened, only curiously peaceful. As I sat there staring at him, I began to feel curiously peaceful myself, as though he must soon wake up refreshed by such deep sleep and we should all be happy again.

The minutes seemed like hours and Terry did not move. Still I sat watching and wondering. Perhaps Terry was already dead! The thought made me feel cold and sick, and once again my eyes filled with frightened tears. If only Philip would come back! What was death, in any case? And if Terry were dead, where had he gone? We should bury his quiet little body under the ground in the churchyard, but would that really be Terry? Or would Terry have gone to heaven, like we sang about in hymns in church? But would Terry be happy? One grubby, rather naughty little boy, amongst all those golden streets and white wings!

Then I suddenly remembered Jane Collins, who had gone "to be with the Lord", and the radiant face of the child in my dream. Perhaps dying just meant going to live with the Shepherd and hearing him speak with our proper ears and seeing him with real eyes, instead of just inside our hearts. That would be lovely, I thought. No wonder the little girl had looked so happy. And perhaps that was why Terry looked so peaceful.

But Terry did not know about the Good Shepherd, so perhaps he might not be so pleased to go and live with him. I was sure Terry had never heard anything about it all. If only I'd had a chance to tell him! If he didn't die I should tell him at once, and then Philip and he and I would all belong together. But anyhow, even if he were dead, I was sure that the Good Shepherd would see that he was happy in heaven. Because, after all, it wasn't Terry's fault that he had never asked to be found and forgiven. It was really mine, because I had kept the secret to myself instead of sharing it.

So I sat hugging my knees, with my eyes fixed on Terry's still face, torn between hope and fear. Every few minutes I thought I heard Philip coming back, but each time it turned out to be only a rabbit, or a bird, or a gust of wind in the trees. The sunshine streamed through the thin, vivid foliage of the larches and rested in a bright patch on Terry's hair, almost as though God were touching him, I thought to myself. And I remembered how in the Gospel of Luke, which I read every morning, the Saviour had touched men and women and children who were hurt and ill, and they always got well again at once.

"Oh God," I whispered, looking up through the branches, "please make Terry better. Don't let him die. We want him here so much. Amen."

It was then that I heard Philip's voice through the trees and some men's voices talking too. A moment later a little procession came into sight with Philip leading the way. Behind him came Uncle Peter, who was always at home on Saturdays, and kind Doctor Paterson who had come to see me when I had measles. Behind them came two men in a dark uniform carrying a stretcher; I heard later that these were the ambulance men.

Dr Paterson knelt down at once and put his fingers on Terry's wrist. He held it for a long time and then passed his hands over Terry's head, drew back his eyelids, and bent his legs and arms backwards and forwards very gently. Then he turned to me.

"Has the boy moved since he fell?" he asked.

"No," I answered, "he's been as though he was fast asleep all the time." Then, emboldened by the sound of my own voice, I gave the doctor's coat a little tug. "Is he dead?" I whispered.

"No," the doctor answered gently, "he's not dead, but he's very badly hurt. You were a good girl to stay here alone and look after him. Now we'll take him along to the hospital as soon as we can, and I'm going to see what I can do for him."

Very gently and carefully Terry was lifted on to the stretcher, and the men set off through the brambles with the precious burden beneath them. Uncle Peter, seeing how white and scared I looked, stooped down and picked me up in his arms like a baby. I snuggled up against him, laid my throbbing head on his shoulder, and felt greatly comforted. I had always been good friends with Uncle Peter.

But I noticed Philip's face only when he glanced towards me, for he had walked with his head turned sideways. He said nothing, but his lips were pressed tightly together and his eyes were desperate. They reminded me of the eyes of a rabbit I had once found caught in a trap. His cheeks, high up, were scarlet, but the rest of his face was quite white. In that moment I realised that all my uncertain fears were nothing up to Philip's misery. I longed to run and comfort him, but knew that there was nothing I could say or do. Nothing would comfort him except Terry getting well.

We all walked very slowly so as not to jolt the stretcher, for the ground was rough and uneven. We took a narrow, overgrown path which led on to the road, and the hazel bushes brushed my face as I lay in Uncle Peter's arms. The ambulance was waiting there, and Dr Paterson climbed in with Terry while the men sat in front.

"When will you tell us if he's better?" I asked, just as he was about to shut the door.

"I shall be passing your house tomorrow," said the doctor "and I'll drop in and let you know."

The door was shut and the engine started up. The ambulance sped off in a cloud of white dust, and Uncle

Peter, Philip and I were left to trudge home. Uncle asked us a few questions about Terry on the way, but otherwise we were very silent. Nobody felt like talking.

It was a long, wretched day. We hung about the garden unable to settle down to anything, and with no appetite for our meals. Aunt Margaret felt sorry for us and read aloud to us after tea, but we were both glad when bedtime arrived. She came upstairs and kissed us goodnight, but as soon as her footsteps had died away I hopped out of bed and over to Philip. He was lying huddled up in bed, and I think he had been crying, for his voice sounded sniffy and his pillow was damp. I got under the rug at the bottom and curled myself up in a ball like a kitten.

"Ruth," whispered Philip, rather shakily, "do you think he'll die?"

"No," I answered decidedly, "I don't."

"Why not?" asked Philip, rather surprised at my being so sure of myself. "Did Dr Paterson say anything to you when I wasn't listening?"

I wriggled my bare toes up and down under the rug, as I always did when I was shy. It was difficult to explain, but I thought now was the moment to try and tell.

"Well, you see," I answered, "when you'd gone to get the others, I prayed to God very hard that Terry would get better again, so I expect he will."

Philip stared at me over the top of the sheet.

"So did I," he admitted, slowly. "I said, 'Oh God, please don't let Terry die', all the way home, but I don't know whether it was much use. I'm not a very good boy and I usually forget to say my prayers altogether, and nothing much happens when I do."

"But Philip," I said, uncurling myself, and sitting up straight, because I was so very much in earnest, "you don't have to be a specially good person to say your prayers. You just have to belong to the Shepherd. That's what my secret was, that I was going to tell you about today. I didn't make it up. Mr Robinson told me when I ran away, and it's in the Bible too. When we're naughty we're like sheep that run away and get lost, and can't find the way back. But Jesus is the Shepherd. He comes to look for us, and when we ask him, he finds us. But he always waits till we ask. Then we belong to him and he listens to everything we say, and he speaks to us and tells us how to be good. Mr Tandy told me all about listening to his voice. And Jesus spoke to me last night and stopped me from losing my temper with Aunt Margaret, when she wouldn't let me have a chocolate biscuit."

I could see Philip staring at me, his face pale in the moonlight. "Go on," he said.

"There's not much more to say," I continued, "except that when Terry was lying on the ground the sun suddenly shone through the trees right on to his hair, and I thought perhaps it was God's way of touching him and making him better, like Jesus touched people in the Bible. And after that I was almost sure he wasn't going to die."

There was a long silence, broken at last by Philip.

"Did you ask Jesus to find you?" he asked, curiously.

I nodded. "I did it on the way home," I said, "in the primrose woods. I asked him to forgive me for being naughty, and to find me and make me one of his lambs as Mr Robinson said. Oh, Philip, I wish you would come with me and see that clergyman, because he'd tell you about it much better than me, and I do so want you to belong to the Shepherd, too."

"I wish I did," said Philip in a small sober voice. "Do you think I could?"

"I'm sure you could," I answered, very decidedly. "I should think you'd be much easier to find than me because you're so much gooder. I don't think you'd take much finding at all."

But Philip shook his head. "You don't know," he said sadly. "You only see me outside. I'm not at all good inside."

"Well," I argued, "it doesn't matter. I'll show you my picture and you'll see. The sheep there is nearly falling over a precipice, he's got so lost, but the shepherd is going to find him all the same."

I tiptoed across the passage and returned with my precious picture in my hand. We both went over to the window, and could see it quite clearly because the full moon was shining right in at the window. Philip went on looking at it for a long time.

"Could I ask now, Ruth?" he said at last, rather anxiously.

I nodded.

"Then you must go away," he explained, "because I shall have to be alone. We'll talk more about it in the morning."

So I left him, with his elbows on the windowsill, looking at the near hills. I snuggled into bed and stared up sleepily at the millions of stars.

# 11

# A visit to the vicarage

The rest of the holidays passed all too quickly because there was so much to do. The doctor came to see us next day. As soon as we heard his car stop, we flung ourselves out of the gate, and nearly knocked him backwards in our eagerness to hear the news.

"Steady, steady!" exclaimed Dr Paterson, collaring us both. "If you knock me out I shan't be able to tell you anything."

Terry was alive, he told us, but he had hurt his back and head very badly indeed, and would be in hospital many weeks. His mother was with him nearly all the time now. But as soon as he was a little better he should probably be moved to another hospital – a special hospital for people with broken bones. We could not go and visit him because it was too far away, but we should probably be able to write to him in a few weeks' time.

This was quite enough to calm our fears and make us happy again. Terry was alive and being looked after. He would certainly get better soon, we told ourselves, just as we had always got better in time from measles and colds and tummy-aches. So we stopped worrying, and settled down to enjoy the last few days of the holidays as much as we could.

We decided that we must pay one last visit to each of our friends. So Philip went to call on the bird man, and was taken down to see a moorhen's nest, and I paid a visit to Mr Tandy in the sheepfolds. But there wasn't much time for conversation, because Mr Tandy was busy shearing.

The last day of all we set apart for visiting the clergyman, and we set out about half-past three, because we thought it would be rather nice to arrive about teatime.

The village lay at the bottom of the hill, and we marched in at the vicarage gate, very sure of a welcome. We did not have to walk far, for my friend was in his shirtsleeves mowing the lawn, and recognised me at once. He seemed delighted to see us both. He did not even ask us if we would stay to tea. He simply said, "You've both arrived just at the right moment." It certainly seemed as though we had, for no sooner had I introduced Philip than Mrs Robinson, the clergyman's wife, appeared on the lawn with a tea tray. From the way Mr Robinson rushed indoors and fetched jam tarts and chocolate spread, you might almost have thought that we were expected!

We had a lovely tea. Mr and Mrs Robinson sat in deckchairs and we sat on a rug and ate a tremendous lot. Then we both told Mr Robinson all about our special secret. He was so pleased, His face just looked like Mr Tandy's when I'd told him, and he began to talk to us about reading our Bible.

"We'll do it together," I said eagerly, "shan't we, Philip?" But before he could answer, Mrs Robinson appeared at the window.

"Twins' bedtime, Ruth," she called. "Do you want to come and watch?"

I jumped up. "Will you excuse me, please, Mr Robinson?" I said, a little anxiously, for I did not wish him to think me rude.

"Certainly," he replied. "You go. My wife will be glad of some help. Philip and I will stay here a little longer, and do some more talking."

I sped across the lawn, and into the vicarage. The twins were crawling about on the carpet while their mother collected their night things. They were 10 months old and very lively, and I, who had never had anything to do with babies, thought I had never seen anything to equal them.

I spent a glorious half hour. Once they were safely in the big bath, Mrs Robinson let me soap their plump little bodies and then pour the water all over them. Then we sailed a yellow sponge duck, and the twins screamed with laughter and beat the water with their fat hands. I was allowed to sprinkle sweet-smelling powder into their folds and creases. And, when they were safely in their nightgowns, I was given a soft little hairbrush with which I brushed their hair up on end. It was not proper hair at all. It was more like yellow chicken down that rolled itself into sausage-curls down the middle of their heads. And all the time I was doing it they wriggled, and chuckled, and tried to bite their toes.

It was not till their mother was tucking them firmly into their cots that I noticed the picture that hung on the wall behind them. It was another picture of the Good Shepherd, but it was different from mine. This shepherd was standing by a lake, with his hand stretched out to bless the little lambs that stood beside him and lay asleep at his feet.

It was an evening picture, and it reminded me of the lambs in Mr Tandy's sheepfold, when the sun sank behind the bluebell woods and the shadows crept up the fields.

"Oh!" I cried joyfully, pointing up at it. "I've got a Good Shepherd picture, too, but it's not like that. My sheep is on a precipice."

"I know your picture," answered Mrs Robinson, "and I love it very much, and later I shall show it to the twins. But they are not old enough to understand anything about precipices yet. I like to think that all through the night, when I'm asleep, the Good Shepherd is looking after my babies for me. So I put that picture there to remind me, and whenever I look at it I remember they are perfectly safe."

I stared at the twins. They had both fallen asleep instantly. Janet had curled herself up and had stuffed two fingers into her mouth. Robin lay on his back with his arms thrown out on the pillow, his cheeks flushed with the warmth of sudden deep sleep.

I looked up into Mrs Robinson's face. "Can I come again?" I whispered.

"Of course you can," she replied. "You can come on Saturday week if your aunt will let you. I'll write and ask her. We'll take the twins out in the pram, and then you can help me give them their supper and put them to bed. It's a great treat for me to have a helper, and I can see that you're handy with babies."

I felt myself blush with pride. "Oh yes, I shall love to come. I can come, I know I can." I couldn't exactly have Mrs Robinson for my mother, but perhaps in time I might become a sort of elder sister to the twins.

On returning to the garden I found Mr Robinson and Philip deep in conversation. I was eager to get back and ask my aunt about Saturday week. My delight was doubled when Mr Robinson said that Philip might come too and help him in the garden, and we'd all have tea together. Saturday afternoon was Mr Robinson's weekly holiday and he said we should always find him at home.

We got back in good time for supper, and I ran straight off to my aunt.

"Auntie," I cried, hopping about on one foot, "Mrs Robinson has invited me to tea with her on Saturday week – her and the babies – and I can push the pram and put them to bed. I can go, can't I? Do say yes!"

My aunt looked rather annoyed.

"Who is this Mrs Robinson, Ruth?" she asked, rather coldly. "You are not to visit people without consulting me. I have never heard of the lady."

"Oh, she's quite all right, Auntie," I assured her, anxiously. "She's a very nice lady indeed, a clergyman's wife at Fairways. She's going to write to you."

"I should hope so," retorted my aunt, "but I'm afraid the answer will have to be no this time, because Miss Montgomery called this afternoon to say that her little niece was coming to stay. I said that you would go and play with her that afternoon. I'm sorry you should be disappointed, but perhaps this Mrs Robinson will invite you another day. If she is really the wife of the vicar of Fairways, I have no objection to your accepting. I have heard they are very nice people."

I flew into a rage at once.

"But Auntie," I stormed, "you know that I *hate* going to tea with Miss Montgomery. And I *hate* Juliana Montgomery – she's like a little white mouse. She doesn't know how to play anything nice, and we have to sit indoors and play dominoes, and I *hate* dominoes. Oh, *please*, Auntie, say I needn't visit Juliana. I told Mrs Robinson I could come!"

"Then you had no business to tell Mrs Robinson," replied my aunt, sharply. "I never heard such nonsense! You are never to accept invitations without my permission. And stand still while you talk. You are making me quite dizzy."

But I had thoroughly lost my temper by this time, and was nearly crying with disappointment.

"I won't go!" I shouted. "I shall go where I like. I told Mrs Robinson I'd come, and I shall, and you shan't stop me!"

My aunt took hold of my arm.

"Go straight to bed," she said, firmly. "Don't let me hear any more of this rudeness. I thought you were going to try and improve, but this does not look like improvement at all. Off you go!"

I shook myself free and marched off with my head in the air.

"I don't care," I muttered over my shoulder, and slammed the door behind me as hard as I could.

But I *did* care – very much indeed! Almost before I'd reached the top of the stairs, I'd realised what I'd done, and by the time I crept into bed I thought my heart was breaking. I curled up in a ball, buried my face in the pillow, and wept and wept.

I had forgotten to listen to the voice of the Good Shepherd. Perhaps he would never speak to me again. Perhaps he would stop loving me. Perhaps I should even stop belonging to him, and then there would be no one to help me to be good. Oh, why hadn't I waited and listened?

"Ruth, what *is* the matter? You mustn't cry like this!"

I had been sobbing so bitterly that I never heard my aunt come in. I turned around quickly and swallowed down my tears, for I did not really want her to see how sorry I was. She was sitting by my bed, and she had a glass of milk and a plate of biscuits in her hand.

"What is the matter, Ruth?" she asked again, and her voice was rather anxious, for she had never seen me cry like that before.

I tried to answer in my ordinary voice, but could not manage it. I buried my head afresh in the pillow and began crying again.

I did not want to tell her, but it suddenly occurred to me that she might be able to answer my questions, and I wanted to know the answer so badly that I blurted it all out.

"It's the Shepherd," I sobbed. "I lost my temper and perhaps I shan't belong to him any more. Oh, Auntie, do you think I shall be able to come back to him, if I'm good next time?"

I lifted my face in my eagerness to hear her answer, but she was staring at me as if I had lost my senses.

"What *are* you talking about, Ruth?" she asked, helplessly.

I dived for the chair and found my picture in my Bible. I pulled it out, and held it in front of her with a great sniff and a gulp.

"That," I answered. "You see, I was his sheep, but I forgot to listen, and perhaps he'll never speak to me again, because I lost my temper so badly. Do you think, Auntie, he'd forgive me just this once?"

My aunt was staring very hard at the picture, and she didn't speak for a long time.

"Who gave you this picture, Ruth?" she asked at last.

"Mr Robinson, the clergyman," I replied, "and he told me all about it. You know the story, don't you, Auntie? Do you think Jesus will forgive me, Auntie, if I never, never do it again?"

She was still staring at the picture and the answer was a long time in coming.

"Auntie," I whispered impatiently, giving her arm a little shake, "do you think he might?"

"If you are really sorry for being naughty, and are determined to try and be different, I am quite sure God will forgive you. You had better ask him."

My aunt stayed with me while I ate, but we said very little. When I had finished, she kissed me goodnight and left me very drowsy and quite comforted. But before I fell asleep, I buried my face in the pillow again, and breathed out a prayer for forgiveness to the One who stood close beside me, and who cared equally for lost lambs, fallen sparrows, sleeping babies, and bad little girls.

# 12

# We get a letter

The summer term sped by. Philip went crazy over cricket and we spent long happy evenings on the common bowling overs to each other. Philip's school was a good way off and he had no friends from our part of the district. And I never wanted to have anything to do with the other girls from my school when Philip was about.

The baby birds we had watched and loved were all fledged and out in the world by now, and the nests deserted. But early in the mornings we often climbed the hills to watch the larks spring up from the bracken and soar, singing, up into the sunrise. Then we would race home to breakfast, leaping over the rocks and gorse bushes, shouting to each other as we ran, so that the sheep fled away from us and the ravine between the hills echoed with the sound of our voices.

The summer holidays had come round again before we heard from Terry. All the summer he had been in a children's hospital in Birmingham, and from time to time we got news of him from Dr Paterson. We wrote to him quite a lot and told him all about the woods, what flowers were coming out, and what birds we had seen, but he never answered. So it was a great surprise when the postman, meeting us at the gate one morning, handed us a letter addressed to us.

Nobody but Father or Mother ever wrote to us, and this was certainly not their writing. It was larger, and shaky, and looked as though the writer was not very used to writing letters at all.

"Dear Filip and Ruth," it ran, "I am come home but I has to stop in bed. Please come and see me from Terry my adress is Willow Cottage, The Hollow, Tanglewoods."

We were so impatient to start that we could scarcely eat our dinner, and we talked about it all the time. My aunt seemed slightly doubtful when we showed her the note, but said we could go all the same.

"I only hope it's a clean cottage, and that you won't catch anything. Don't stay too long, will you?"

As soon as dinner was over, we raced to our rooms to hunt in our drawers, for we wanted to take Terry a present. I found a bar of chocolate and Philip found a catapult, so we wrapped them up in separate parcels and put them in our pockets. Then we hurled ourselves out of the front door and set off for Tanglewoods. Tanglewoods was such a little village that it was really quite difficult to tell when you got there. There was a public house called the Goat and Compasses. A long way further down the road was a shop which sold groceries and candles and cattle food and medicine and cough mixtures, and had a post office in one corner. Further on still was a tiny church with some old tombstones falling backwards. But none of these by themselves could be called the village, for the real Tanglewoods consisted of scattered farms and cottages resting on the flanks of the low hills, and of barns and outhouses hidden among the hop yards. No one knew where Tanglewoods started, and no one knew where it ended, so Terry's address took us some time to trace.

We came through the woods, and down over the ridge where swathes of hay from the late second mowing lay in tidy rows up the meadows. The view in front reminded us of a patchwork quilt, with its dark green hop yards, golden cornfields ripe for harvesting and its pink stretches where willow herb grew in rosy clusters. Everywhere we looked we saw risings and hollows and little hills and valleys, and we stood for a while trying to guess in which particular hollow Terry lived.

There was no one in sight, and we made for the nearest farm to ask the way. We found a woman churning in a cool stone dairy. She came to the door, and pointed further down the valley.

"You'll be meaning that tumbledown place down Sheep's Hollow. There's a gypsy sort of woman lives there with a boy. She's been up here begging many times. Follow the track down through the gorse bushes, and then follow the brook. It leads right down into the hollow."

We thanked her and passed on, and she stood staring after us curiously as though she would have liked to know our business at Willow Cottage. But we did not want to be delayed or stopped, and we hurried down the hill as fast as we could. Then we saw the cottage in the hollow lying just below us, with its broken chimney pot and the holes in the roof where slates had blown off.

It was a dark little hollow that had once been part of a quarry, although the clematis had covered up the bare rocks and made a green curtain round its sides. The stream trickled through it in a stagnant, slimy ooze, and we wondered why anyone should have chosen to build a cottage in such a damp, cheerless spot, when there was all the open hillside to choose from. But we learned later from Terry that it had been built as a hut for storing dynamite for the quarry, and only later made into a house.

It looked so desolate and deserted, with its broken windows stuffed with rag, and the nettles growing round the door, that we hung back half-frightened. Surely Terry couldn't live here! But even as we stood hesitating at the entrance of the hollow, the door opened and a woman appeared and stood staring back at us.

She was a big, powerful woman with tanned skin and black, untidy hair gathered back in her handkerchief. Her face was hard and unhappy and she looked at us as if she disliked us.

Nobody spoke for a moment or two. Then the woman broke the silence.

"Well," she asked, "what be you kids a-wanting here?"

We came forward slowly.

"Please," explained Philip, "Terry wrote us a letter to come and see him, so we came. Please, we're so glad that he's well enough to come home."

The woman's face still looked hard.

"Be you the children as was with my Terry when he fell?" she asked, suspiciously.

"Yes," we answered, rather guiltily.

"You didn't ought to have let him done it," she muttered. "Still, he's been carrying on something awful about you two coming to see 'im, so you'd best come in."

She jerked the door back roughly and led the way inside. We followed, but I slipped my hand into Philip's and held it tight. The little room into which she entered was gloomy, hot and airless, and there was a strange smell, too, that made me want to sneeze. There was only one little window, and it was too high to see through it.

But a moment later we had forgotten all this, and had both run forward with a cry of welcome. For on the bed in the corner lay Terry, and we had not seen him for three and a half months.

He did not smile at us, for his face had grown so sullen and unhappy that he looked as though he hardly knew how to smile. But he held out his hand and remarked gravely that he was real pleased to see us, and he'd been looking out for us ever since morning.

We said equally gravely that we were very pleased to see him, and then there was a long silence because none of us could think of anything to say at all.

Philip broke it at last by asking how Terry had enjoyed hospital.

"'Tweren't bad," Terry admitted, "but I got browned off with lying so still like, and nothing to look at but them streets. And here 'tis just as bad – nothing to look at but that there wall. The window be too high up to see out of. And if I could, there'd be nothing to see 'cept the side of the hollow."

"But couldn't we carry your bed outside?" I asked, looking doubtfully at the heavy iron bedstead on which he lay.

He shook his head.

"Couldn't get it through the door without taking it to pieces," he replied gloomily, "and yer can't move me off it. Me back hurts too bad."

"Haven't you any books?" we asked.

"I ain't much good at reading," he answered, "although maybe I'd enjoy 'em if they'd pictures in. What I wants to see is them hills and birds and animals, and things."

His voice shook a little, and his big eyes filled with tears. Poor, tired, cross little Terry! We both felt very sorry for him, and didn't know how to comfort him.

"I'll bring you all my bird books," said Philip, who was looking most upset. "We'll come ever so often and tell you what things are looking like, and then when we're gone, you can shut your eyes and pretend you're seeing them. I'll tell you what Tanglewoods looks like now, when we came over the hills this afternoon. They haven't got in the second mowings yet, so the hay is still lying out in the fields, and the willow herb patches are just beginning to turn woolly. The hops will soon be ripe and are beginning to smell when you go past the yards, and the apples in the orchard are beginning to turn rosy and weigh down the branches. Oh, and I think they will cut the harvests very soon because the wheat is ripe and the wind makes nice noises in it. I saw Mr Lake getting out his tractor. And there are lots of flowers – scabious, and poppies, and knapweeds, and bedstraws and things. We'll bring you some round next time, and some apples."

Terry seemed pleased. A faint tinge of colour crept into his almost white cheeks.

"You goin' to the hop fields?" he asked wistfully.

"We might," I answered, "if Auntie will let us. We could earn some money then, couldn't we, Philip? To help with the camera."

"I used to earn a heap of money down at the hop yards," said Terry. "Nuff to buy me a pair of winter boots. Mum'll have to try and go this year, but she can't leave me long, and she's had to give up her work to stop and mind me."

"The gypsies are arriving already," I went on eagerly. "I saw them putting up camp outside a lovely little yellow caravan, with lots of little children with black hair tumbling up and down the steps. They're camping in Mr Lake's field. I'd love to be a gypsy, wouldn't you?"

But Terry, who knew much more than I did about gypsies, shook his head darkly.

"You be thankful fer what yer are," he advised, wisely.

We found no further difficulty in thinking of things to say. Indeed, we talked so much that we stayed much longer than we meant to, and were interrupted by Terry's mother bringing his tea.

Terry's meal consisted of a cup of very strong tea and a crust thinly spread with margarine, on a chipped old plate. It did not look at all appetising to me, but it reminded me of the chocolate I'd brought. It had begun to melt rather, in my pocket, but it was still very nice, and Terry's eyes absolutely gleamed when he saw it. We did not give him the catapult because it did not seem as though it would be any use. His arms looked too thin and white to aim with it.

"Terry," asked Philip just as we were leaving, "when are you going to be able to get up and play with us again?"

Terry did not answer for a minute, but the frightened, unhappy look came back into his eyes.

"Maybe never," he whispered. "They thinks I don't know, but down at the 'ospital I 'eard the doctor talking to the nurse, and 'e said, 'It's all up with 'im, poor little chap! I can't do nuffing more for 'im.' And I think maybe that's why they let my mum take me 'ome. They can't do nuffing more to make me better."

We were horrified to hear this, and once again we could think of nothing to say to comfort poor Terry. So we left him rather sadly. But, just as we were going out of the door, he called after us.

"When yer comin' again?"

"We can't come tomorrow," answered Philip, "because we've got to go to the dentist. But we'll come the day after and bring the bird books."

"For certain sure?" called Terry.

"For certain sure," we called back.

Terry's mother was out in the hollow hanging up a torn little nightshirt on the clothes line. She gave us a surly glance, but did not speak. When we said goodbye she only grunted.

"What a cross woman!" I remarked, as we climbed the hollow. "I'm glad she's not my mother."

But on the whole we were very silent on the way home, because we were both feeling so sorry for Terry and we were both wondering what we could do to make his life happier. Nothing we could think of seemed much good, because nothing could make up for having to lie all day in a dark, stuffy room, staring at the wall, while the apples ripened and the harvest fields rustled outside.

# 13

# A moonlight expedition

We went to see Terry very often during the next few weeks, and I believe now that it was only our visits that kept him alive through those long dark days when he lay flat on his aching back, staring at the wall. Philip lent him all his most precious nature books, and we took him all the chocolate we had, and baskets of fruit from the orchard. We felt well rewarded every time by the faint flush of pleasure on his white cheeks and the flicker of happiness that would light up his eyes. He never thanked us in words, and his mother still stared at us as though she hated us. But we knew, nevertheless, that Terry's waking hours were spent wondering if we would come, and that he lay from dinnertime onwards with his eyes fastened on the door and his ears straining for the sound of our footsteps.

We had told Aunt Margaret about him, and once or twice she had sent him little presents. Aunt Margaret and I were slowly getting to understand each other, and I no longer tried to wriggle out of helping her in the mornings. At first I had done my jobs because I thought I ought to. But after a few days I found that housework was really quite fun, as long as I was doing my best and not trying to get out of it all the time. My aunt said nothing, but I knew she was pleased at the change. Gradually we grew fond of each other and I began to talk to her more freely, instead of keeping everything a secret from her.

Uncle Peter was interested in Terry, too. Once or twice he had taken the stepladder to the orchard and picked the enormous rosy apples that grew right at the top of the tree against the sky, for us to take to him. They were the size of big grapefruits. When they were polished up we could see our faces in their shiny skins. Terry loved them, and even his mother looked interested.

"Did yer pick those there in your garden?" she asked suddenly one afternoon, as we placed one of them between his small white hands.

We quite jumped, for except for her first greeting it was the first time she had ever spoken to us. We turned smiling towards her, for we wanted her to come to like us as much as Terry did.

"Yes," I answered, "we've lots of trees full of big, shiny apples like these. We shall be picking them in about a week, and then we'll bring some more. But we picked these early because we thought Terry would like them."

She only grunted and turned away, but I could not help feeling pleased she had spoken to us and admired our apples. I thought I would try and talk to her again another day.

The nights just then were very hot, and it did not get dark until very late. Philip and I used to kick our bedclothes on to the floor and lie in our night things by the open windows trying to get cool. Often I got tired of lying alone, and would go and sit on his bed. We would talk until the cool darkness gathered round us and we felt ready for sleep.

It was on one of these hot, still nights, when the sky was still red with the last glow of sunset, that I tiptoed across the passage and stuck my head out of the window beside him. A breath of air seemed to move towards us from the hills, bringing with it the cry of a sheep somewhere up among the rocks.

"I don't think I shall be able to go to sleep all night, Phil," I remarked. "It's such a beautiful night I seem to want to look out of the window all the time. It's a full moon, too. Look, I can see it coming up behind that fir tree."

We watched it climb above the horizon, almost blood-red in colour. It seemed all tangled up in the black boughs of the fir, but soon it would steer clear and all the world would be flooded with soft silver light. I turned suddenly to Philip, my head full of moonlight.

"Phil!" I whispered excitedly. "Have you ever been out on the hills at night?"

"No," answered Philip, "I haven't. Not proper night. Why?"

"Oh, Philip," I breathed, giving his arms a little squeeze, "let's go now, just out through the hedge and up above the quarry. It would be so beautiful, just you and me, and the big yellow moon. Come on, Phil!"

Philip hesitated. "Do you think it would be very naughty?" he asked. "After all, you know, we were going to try to be good these holidays."

"I know," I urged. "And we really have been good, too. At least, I've been cross with Aunt Margaret once or twice, but last holidays I was cross nearly every day. And it isn't really a bit naughty either. After all, what's naughty in wanting to see the moon? It's not hurting anyone and it's not even being disobedient, because Aunt Margaret has never actually told us not to go out at night and look at the moon."

Philip thought this over for a minute or two. It seemed to strike him as sensible, for all he said was, "Are you going to dress properly?"

"Oh, no," I said, "I shan't bother. I shall tuck my nightie up and put on my mack. You put on your best trousers, those long ones, over your pyjamas, and put on your mack, too."

This was no sooner said than done and, looking rather lumpy about the lower quarters, with our handkerchiefs stuffed in our mouths because we wanted to giggle, Philip and I tiptoed down to the front door and turned the key. It creaked and grated alarmingly, but my uncle and aunt must have been very soundly asleep, for although we stood rooted to the spot for several moments, nothing happened.

We shut the door noiselessly behind us and stepped out into the open. Then we both stopped and looked round, because the world seemed so strange and different, and the sky, with its millions of stars, looked so far away. I slipped my hand into Philip's as I always did when things seemed strange, and together we tiptoed through the shadowed orchard towards our gap. The shadows of the apple boughs looked so fierce and frightening that I almost ran back. Only Philip, having made up his mind, kept going.

Out through the gap and up the stony track that led to the hills we went without a word. Up the steps behind the clock tower, over the first group of grey rocks, and we were there, standing on the lower slopes by moonlight, with the silver world lying at our feet.

"Come on!" whispered Philip and, seizing my hand again, he began to climb.

We climbed in silence until we reached the very top of the North Hill and stood by the little cairn of stones that marked the summit. The wind came sweeping up the valleys, clean and pure, and laden with the scents of gorse and bracken. A sheep lifted its head at the sound of our footsteps and bleated a warning to the stars. Otherwise all was silent and we sat down on the cairn to look.

There was such a tremendous lot to see in spite of the darkness. Behind, there were the black shapes of the hills and in front of us stretched the plains dotted with points of light. Every river and pond gleamed in the moonlight like some silver fairy lake.

But mostly we looked up because we both loved stars, and tonight they all shone clearly, right over the vast panorama of the sky.

We stayed quite a long time, until Philip remarked that he thought we'd better get back, as it would soon be morning and we should be so tired next day. Actually it was not quite as bad as that, for when we reached the bottom of the hill, the clock on the tower struck one, and nearly made us jump out of our skins.

We sang all the way down because we knew there was no one to hear us, and it was a relief to make a noise after that tremendous solitude. We sang all the songs we could remember, mostly about seas and ships and one about a mermaid who lured mariners to their death. While we sang, we jumped over the gorse bushes, or leaped from one rock to the other like two mountain goats.

But when we got back to the stony track we suddenly felt tired and thought how nice it would be to cuddle down into bed and go to sleep.

"Now," said Philip, "in through the gap and very, very quietly across the orchard. How awful if Auntie noticed us! We must absolutely creep."

We were right through the gap and well into the orchard when Philip suddenly stopped dead and dug his fingernails into my arm. With the other hand he pointed, and as I followed his finger my heart seemed to turn right over, and I only just stopped myself from screaming.

# 14

# A night-time adventure

A tall figure in a dark cloak was moving towards us through the trees, bowed under the weight of a sack.

She had not seen us, for we had come very quietly, and we stood hidden in the deep shadows of the apple trees. But the figure was making for the gap and, in a few minutes, must pass right by where we stood. I think I should have fainted outright if it had not been for Philip, who seemed less frightened than I was.

"It's a woman stealing apples," he breathed. "We ought to try and stop her. They're Auntie's apples and she's got a great big sackful."

I could not argue or tell him to stop, because I was much too scared to speak. But I clung tightly to Philip and was sort of dragged with him when he suddenly stepped out into the open to confront the figure, who was nearly upon us. The moonlight shone full on her face, and we recognised her in a flash. It was Terry's mother!

She gave a short, terrified shriek and dropped the sack, so that the apples rolled out and scattered in all directions. Then she cowered down in the grass, and covered her face with her cloak and began mumbling words very fast, almost as though she was saying her prayers. Neither

Philip nor I knew what to do, until she suddenly flung back her fierce, proud head and spoke to us.

"So ye'd be a-spying on me by night even, would ye?" she hissed, shaking her fist at us. "And now ye'll be sending the police after me tomorrer and they'll take me from my poor dyin' boy. You, with yer fine food, and yer grand clothing, yer can't spare the price of a few apples for my laddie what's starvin' and cold, and him a-dyin' before my very eyes, and me with nothing ter give him – oh! Terry, Terry, they'll take me from you!" She hid her face in her cloak again and burst into bitter, passionate weeping.

I looked at Philip, feeling more troubled than I had ever felt before. Philip was frowning, too, as though he was wondering what to do next. Presently, however, he made up his mind, for he suddenly squatted down in the grass beside the poor huddled up figure, and tried to draw her hands from her face.

"We weren't spying on you," he said, gently, "we were only here by accident, because we wanted to see the moon."

The woman had stopped sobbing, and was looking intently at him, with a gleam of hope in her wild eyes.

"Little gentleman," she answered in a trembling voice, taking hold of him in her eagerness, "listen to me! I swear before God I'll never come again. I know I'm a bad woman and I didn't oughter have come, but my Terry's a-dyin' and the doctor, he says to me, you get 'im extra milk and a warm blanket for the winter, and you feed 'im up proper if you want to keep him a little longer. And my Terry, he's all that I've got."

She was kneeling in the grass, clasping her hands almost as though she was praying to us.

I wanted to assure her that of course we wouldn't tell, and she could have all the apples she wanted, because I felt so sorry for her, but Philip stopped me.

"We won't tell anyone," he said slowly, "but if you really stop stealing, as you say, I can't see how you are going to get any money. And yet, it's wrong to steal. Won't anybody give you any money?"

She shook her head.

"If I applied for relief they'd only put Terry back in 'ospital where I couldn't get at 'im. They'd say our house weren't fit for a sick child, and no more 'tis. But we're together. That's wot we wants."

She looked at us hungrily, as though pleading with us to understand. Philip still seemed wrapped in thought.

"Listen!" he said at last, in his most earnest voice. "I think I've got a sort of an idea. But I can't tell you about it now. You go back to Terry, and we'll come and see you tomorrow when we've talked about it. But we've promised not to tell, haven't we, Ruth ?"

"Oh, yes," I agreed, "we won't say anything and we'll come tomorrow."

"God bless you, little lady and gentleman," whispered Terry's mother.

She picked up her empty sack and was gone through the gap in the hedge before we had time to bid her goodnight. We were left alone gazing down at the scattered fruit.

"I wish we'd let her have them," I remarked.

"No," said Philip. "It's Uncle Peter's fruit and it would have been as bad as stealing ourselves if we'd given it to her. I've thought of something else, Ruth, but I'll tell you in the morning. I'm so tired, and I want to go back to bed."

I was very tired, too, so I pressed him with no further questions. We crept upstairs and tumbled into bed. I was just falling asleep when Philip's head came round the door.

"How much is there in the money box?" he whispered.

"One pound 72 pence," I murmured back drowsily, and the next moment I was deep in the land of dreams.

# 15

# About giving

Of course we both overslept next morning and were wakened only by the ringing of the breakfast gong and the sound of my aunt's footsteps coming up to see what had happened to us. She was rather suspicious at the sight of us only just waking up.

"It's my belief you don't settle off properly at night," she remarked severely, "or you'd be awake at the proper time. I believe there's a lot of running about when you should be tucked up, and I won't have it. Once in bed, you're to stay in bed, or I shall have to start locking you in."

Philip and I looked at each other guiltily out of the corners of our eyes, and hoped our aunt would not say any more on the subject. Fortunately it was washing day, and she was very busy, so no more questions were asked.

I was simply longing for a good talk with Philip, but felt that I had really been so naughty the night before, in spite of all my excuses, that I had better try to be extra good today to make up. So I presented myself in the kitchen and offered to turn the mangle and stir the copper, and my aunt was only too pleased to accept. We chatted together in a friendly way while we worked, and I couldn't help thinking how nice it was to have Aunt Margaret talking to me almost as though I was grown up. She never used to do it, and I began to wonder how it was that things were different.

I think it's all to do with the Good Shepherd, I thought to myself as I pegged out the handkerchiefs. It really has been different since Philip and I began to know about him. I do believe he really is beginning to make me less cross and less lazy, and I do believe Aunt Margaret is getting nicer, too. Perhaps after we've been to see Terry this afternoon we might tell Aunt Margaret more about him, and ask her if she has a blanket to spare so he wouldn't be cold in the winter.

"Come along, Ruth!" she called. "Think what you're doing. You've been standing there doing nothing the last three or four minutes."

I felt myself turn red and went on with my work in a great hurry. But I was longing to finish and get to Philip and tell him about my plan and, fortunately for me, the wash was nearly over.

"You can go now," said Aunt Margaret, taking off her apron. "You've been a great help this morning, so you must have a good game before dinner."

I scuttled upstairs two steps at a time, and found Philip lying flat on his bed with all the contents of his money box spread out in front of him. I knelt down and we counted it together.

"One pound 72 pence," observed Philip thoughtfully, "and I saw a camera for four pounds 70 pence. If we both saved our pocket money for the rest of the holidays, we could get it by the beginning of term."

There was a pause, and I watched him anxiously.

"On the other hand," went on Philip, "if we gave Terry 50 pence for extra milk, we could get it round about Christmas."

He gave a little sigh, and I knew he was thinking of the squirrels' dreys and the dormouse nests that we should find when autumn came, and the nests of harvest mice that turned up when the corn was cut.

"Oh, but I don't think we need give 50 pence," I cried. "Surely 25 would buy an awful lot of extra milk, and I vote we ask Auntie for a blanket. She's sure to have an old one."

Philip fingered his coins.

"Well," he said, "I don't think we need really decide now. We can think it out on the way. I'll take the whole money box, and then if I want to give her 25 pence, I can, and if I feel more like 50 pence, I can too!"

I agreed that it was too important a matter to decide in a hurry, and we packed the money back into the box.

We set off after dinner along the well-trodden way that led to Terry's house. I carried a Bible and my picture tucked inside. Philip carried the money box, which was most satisfyingly heavy and jingled as we walked. But he was rather depressed, and I thought he must be thinking about his camera, so I longed to comfort him.

"Philip," I said "I really do think 25 pence might buy quite a lot of extra milk. Let's ask how much extra milk costs."

Philip only grunted. He didn't seem to want to talk about it at all, so we walked on in silence.

We were halfway down the hill towards the hollow when Terry's mother suddenly appeared from behind a tree. She seemed to have been waiting for us. She looked at us very anxiously, as though we might have forgotten our promise.

"Thought we might have our bit of a talk out here," she began nervously, "before you goes on down to Terry. You won't be telling my Terry nothing about them apples, will you now? I did it for his sake, but he'd take on something terrible if he knowed. I don't want 'im finkin' 'is mother is a no-good thief."

"Of course we won't tell Terry," Philip assured her. "We promised we wouldn't tell anyone."

We sat down among the thyme and harebells, and were silent for a little while. Philip looked at me because he was expecting me to begin. I looked at the ground because I was shy, and Terry's mother looked very hard at the money box.

I gave Philip a little kick, but he still wouldn't start talking. Then I thought, what if he took me at my word and gave only 25 pence, when the Good Shepherd had given his life? If only I could make him understand!

Philip moved nearer to Terry's mother.

"We've brought you some money to buy milk and bedclothes for Terry," he said simply. "It's not very much, but it's all we've got," and so saying, he tipped up the money box and emptied the whole contents into Terry's mother's apron.

"It's one pound 72 pence," he said distinctly, so that there might be no mistake about it, "and we hope it will do Terry a lot of good. Now we will go down to the cottage and see him for a little bit."

He stood up and started off down the hill, but I stayed behind for a moment. The Good Shepherd had given his life. Philip had given all the money for his camera. I wanted to give something, too. I suddenly remembered that my most precious possession was in my hands. So I opened the Bible and pulled it out, and laid it with the coins on the black apron.

"It's my picture," I said softly. "And you can have it too. It's the Good Shepherd."

"Thank you, little lady," she replied, and I left her sitting there counting her coins on the hillside, while I ran after Philip.

"I hope you didn't mind that I gave all the money," said Philip apologetically, as we were walking home an hour later. "After all, a lot of it was yours really, but somehow I felt we couldn't keep it. I mean, the camera doesn't seem to matter much compared with Terry, when you come to think of it, does it?"

"No," I agreed, "and the funny part is, I was thinking the same thing. When I thought of the Good Shepherd giving his life, it seemed awful to be giving such a little, and I was trying to make you look at me – to tell you to give more."

"Funny," said Philip, "I thought I should feel miserable without any money, but actually I feel really happy."

"Funny!" I agreed. "I thought it would be terrible giving away my picture, but I sort of feel glad she's got it now. Isn't it odd?"

"Yes," said Philip. "We never guessed it would be so nice. But when you come to think of it, Ruth, I believe it's the first time we've given away anything that we really wanted to keep badly, so we couldn't have known."

And we walked on in silence thinking about it.

# 16

# Hops and mushrooms

The summer holidays were especially exciting that year, because my aunt gave us permission for the first time to spend certain afternoons in the hop fields, where we earned quite a lot of money. We had given up saving for the camera for the present, and our idea was to earn the price of a warm blanket for Terry. We had told Aunt Margaret about it, and this was her suggestion, as she hadn't actually got one to spare herself. But she gave us other little things for him, and mended Philip's old pyjamas, which were flannel and warm and would be much more comfortable than his thin little cotton nightshirts.

Mr Robinson had also promised to go and see Terry. On one of our many Saturday visits, Philip and I had told him about Terry and had begged him to call.

"You see," I'd explained, "I've tried to tell him about the Good Shepherd, but he doesn't want to listen. He says if God loved him he'd make his back better and let him run about again. When he said that, I didn't know what to say. But if you came, you could explain it all nicely, I expect, couldn't you?"

Mr Robinson had smiled.

"No," he'd answered, "I couldn't explain it all, because when God sends sad things into our lives he often doesn't tell us why. He just tells us that it is the best thing for us, and if we really love him we believe what he says even if we don't understand. That is what 'trusting' means. In any case, Terry would probably listen to you more than he would to me, because you are a child like he is and I'm only a grown-up."

"But he doesn't listen," I had insisted. "He doesn't take any notice of me at all. He just tells me to talk about something else."

"Well, then," Mr Robinson had replied, "you must start praying every day that he will listen. God doesn't always answer our prayers at once, but he hears them. And, if they are right prayers, he always answers them in the end. I will come and visit the little boy when I come home from my holiday, and see what I can do for him."

So Mr and Mrs Robinson and the twins had gone off on their holiday and would not be back for three weeks. In the meantime, Philip and I earned what we could in the hop fields. We loved the hop fields with the noisy pickers and the strange smell that clung to our clothes and fingers. We attached ourselves to a family from Birmingham, and listened to their friendly chatter while we picked. At six o'clock, we would line up for our pay and feel wonderfully important and grown up when all our wages were handed out to us.

Once the family from Birmingham invited us to stay to supper with them, and we sat round a glowing brazier. They cooked a strange sort of pancake in a big frying pan. It smelt delicious, and when it was tossed on a tin plate and handed to us we thought we had never tasted anything so good. But Aunt Margaret was cross with us because we got home so late, and when we explained she was crosser still, and said goodness knows what we might catch if we went sitting around braziers and eating off tin plates with gypsies. So that delight had to be given up.

We found another way of earning money, too, which Aunt Margaret thought a better way than hop picking. She was always a little nervous of our catching things or hearing bad language in the hop yards. But one misty morning we got up early and ran out into the silver fields where the spiders were festooning the grasses with their webs. We took off our shoes and stockings because we liked the feel of cold dew between our toes, and were skipping up and down the field, when Philip suddenly stopped. He had caught sight of a little white button mushroom and stooped down to look underneath and make sure it wasn't a puffball.

"Mushrooms, Ruth!" he called. "Let's see if we can find some more!"

We found lots more. In fact, the field was full of them, tight buttons and big umbrellas, and we heaped them up until we could have filled a whole basket full, only we had no basket.

"There's only one thing to be done," Philip remarked. "You must take off your vest and tie the sleeves in a knot so that it makes a bag. We must get these mushrooms home somehow."

When my vest had been filled up with mushrooms it began to stretch, and by the time we reached home it had grown so long that it almost touched the ground. We were going to give some to Aunt Margaret to cook and we were going to ask whether we might sell the rest to the greengrocer up the road.

Aunt Margaret was pleased with the mushrooms, but she was not at all pleased with my vest. She said it was enough to give me a bad chill and, in any case, it was "the ruination of good underwear". So I was given a dose of cold mixture and made to wash the vest, and was rather sulky during breakfast.

But I cheered up later, because when we asked Aunt Margaret if we might sell the rest of our mushrooms to Mr Daniels the greengrocer, she said she did not mind at all, provided we took them in a proper basket. So we set out, highly excited, presented ourselves at the counter, and asked to see Mr Daniels personally.

Mr Daniels was fat and bald, and wore horn-rimmed spectacles on the end of a large red nose. He liked Philip and me, and beamed at us over the counter. When he saw our mushrooms he threw up his hands in admiration.

"Dearie me!" said Mr Daniels. "Now I'll weigh 'em out and pay you same as I pay the farmers. And if you find any more, you bring 'em along to Mr Daniels!"

We did find lots more. What with mushrooms and hops, the money box began to get really heavy again. We were beginning to talk about the colour of the blanket we would buy, when a wonderful thing happened.

We had wandered over the hills in the heat to take Terry some of the Victoria plums, and we found him alone. The cottage was particularly stuffy and Terry looked hot and flushed. His dark hair lay in damp locks on his forehead, and he had thrown all his bedclothes back. He did not notice us come in because he was staring so hard at the wall opposite, where his mother had hung the picture I had given her.

"Hello, Terry!" we greeted him, sitting ourselves down on the bed. "Is your mother out?"

"Mm," answered Terry, wearily. Poor Terry! He seemed so exhausted that even our arrival had failed to cheer him up. "Her's been gone a long time."

"Where to?" we asked.

"Dunno," replied Terry. "Her wouldn't say."

There was a pause, then Terry spoke again in a fretful voice.

"Take that there picture away with you!" he commanded. "It bothers my mum awful. Last few days she's kinder cried when she's looked at it; she was happier before you brought it, and we don't want it."

"But I can't take it away," I objected. "It's your mother's. I gave it to her. It would be sort of stealing to take it away."

Terry passed his hand wearily over his forehead and turned his face to the wall.

"Wish I was dead," he muttered.

We had never seen Terry quite so discouraged before, and we longed to comfort him. But what could we say to comfort a boy who had to lie in this hot, cheerless gloom all day long? Even when we offered him a plum he pushed it away.

"I'm feelin' sick," he explained. "Maybe I'll eat it later."

We left very soon, because he seemed too tired to want us. His mother had not returned, and we felt very depressed as we climbed the hill.

"Philip," I said, "do you still pray every day that Terry will get better?"

"Not *every* day," answered Philip, "because sometimes I feel sure he won't. I mean, perhaps God thinks he'd better not get better. The doctor said he wouldn't, you know, and doctors are usually right."

"But God could do a miracle," I insisted, "like he did in the Bible. It seems too awful, doesn't it? Terry seems sadder every time we go."

"It isn't really being ill that's the worst part," Philip observed thoughtfully, "it's that awful little house. It's so hot and dark, and there's a sort of not very nice smell about it and it must be so dull. If he could be ill somewhere nice it would be different."

But I could see no way out of this difficulty at all, unless we prayed that someone with a nice house would adopt Terry. And, on further thought, we decided not to pray for that after all, as Terry would hate to leave his mother and his mother would hate to lose him.

We were talking so earnestly about it all when we reached the gate that we did not look where we were going and nearly bumped into my aunt. She was coming down the path talking to a tall woman in a dark cloak. We looked up quickly into the visitor's face, and to our utter astonishment we saw that the tall woman was Terry's mother, and her dark eyes were red with weeping. And, stranger still, my aunt, who was generally extremely severe with beggars and gypsies, was talking gently to her and had laid her hand on her arm.

They neither of them took any notice of us, and we went indoors quickly because we somehow felt that Terry's mother hadn't really wanted to meet us at all. But once inside, we looked at each other in astonishment. What could my aunt and Terry's mother have been saying to each other?

"Perhaps she's asking for things for Terry," I suggested.

Philip shook his head.

"I don't think it's that," he said, "because Auntie was being so nice to her, and usually she's rather cross with beggars."

If we had hopes that my aunt would explain things, we were disappointed. She came back into the house a few minutes later and went upstairs to her bedroom. When she came down she was very quiet and took no notice of us at all. I thought her face was sadder than usual and, although she started cooking the supper, she looked as though she was thinking of something that wasn't supper at all.

Next day at breakfast another surprise awaited us. My aunt laid down her knife and fork and looked at her watch.

"Ruth," she announced, "I am going out for the morning. It is very important and I shall probably not be back for some hours, so I am going to let you get the dinner. The potatoes are peeled, and there is cold meat, so you will only have to wash the lettuce, and peel and stew the apples and make some custard. I showed you how to make custard the other day, so it will be a good chance to try."

Philip and I stared at her in astonishment. Never before, that we could remember, had our aunt gone out for the morning, or missed cooking the dinner. It must have been very important business that called her, and we were extremely curious to know what it could be. However, of course, we didn't ask, and I felt so proud at being allowed to cook the dinner all by myself that I soon forgot to wonder.

Aunt Margaret was as good as her word. She got up from the breakfast table, put on her hat, and walked straight out of the front door. And that was the last we saw of her until dinnertime.

Philip and I, left to ourselves, went to work with enthusiasm. Being mistress of the house for the morning rather appealed to me, and we carried the breakfast things out and started to wash up feeling tremendously important. I began by tipping nearly a whole jar of soap flakes into the bowl and whisking until the foam stood up nearly as high as the taps. And after that, of course, we had to spend ten minutes or so scooping it up with our hands and blowing soap bubbles all over the kitchen, squealing with delight as they landed on the top shelves. Then I suddenly remembered that I was not behaving in a very adult way, so I turned to the sink in a great hurry and plunged my elbows into the soapy flakes and began fishing for the silver.

The morning passed very pleasantly. Philip and I peeled enough apples to feed a regiment and, although I burnt our saucepan badly while making the custard, it didn't taste much. We caught three little slugs in the lettuce and carried them carefully back to the lettuce patch in case their mothers should be missing them. Then, when dinner was ready to our satisfaction, we started on the housework. We took all the rugs into the garden and danced up and down with them, smothering ourselves with dust. Yes, it was certainly great fun being left in charge of the house. The morning sped past, and it seemed only a very short time before my aunt walked in at the gate. It was dinnertime.

I made a dive for the potatoes, which were boiling merrily, and the dinner was served up by a very flushed, untidy little cook, who had to be sent away from the table to brush her hair the minute Grace had been said.

However, my aunt seemed pleased with my efforts. She praised the potatoes and salad and said nothing about the burnt flavour of the custard. She looked happy, too – much happier than she had looked at breakfast. And, now and then, we noticed her smiling to herself as though she had some very nice secret.

"I hope you enjoyed yourself this morning, Auntie," said Philip politely.

Aunt Margaret's eyes twinkled, and the little smile played round the corners of her mouth again.

"I've enjoyed myself very much indeed, thank you, Philip," she replied solemnly. Then, after a moment, she added:

"Tonight, when Uncle Peter comes home, and I've talked to him, I'm going to tell you about it. But till then it's a secret."

Philip and I were enormously interested. When evening came we kept running out into the road to see if Uncle was coming. When at last we saw him approaching we tore madly into the kitchen.

"He's coming, Auntie," we shouted, "now, the secret, the secret!"

She shooed us both out of the kitchen with a wooden spoon.

"Get along with you," she said. "I can't make fish cakes and talk secrets at the same time. You tell your uncle to come here, and then you run out into the garden."

So Uncle Peter went in and shut the door.

# 17

# The secret

"Now for the secret!" we exclaimed, and settled ourselves really comfortably on the stools at my aunt's feet.

We were sitting in the summer dusk just outside the French windows, and the air was sweet with the scent of roses, while bats fluttered past on restless wings. My aunt leaned forward in her chair while she talked, and as the story went on, we crept closer and closer until our heads were resting against her knees.

"Well," she said, "before we start talking about secrets, I want to know what you were doing in the orchard at one o'clock in the morning a few weeks ago?"

We both jumped and went very red. This was most unexpected. But, strangely, Auntie did not sound particularly cross. In fact, there was a tiny shake in her voice that might have meant that she was trying not to laugh.

After a very uncomfortable silence, Philip answered in rather a small voice.

"We couldn't go to sleep that night," he explained, "and we wanted to see the moon, and the stars close up. So we put some clothes on and went up to the top of the hill. And then—"

"You went up to the top of the North Hill, alone in the dark?" interrupted my aunt, aghast.

"You've never actually told us not to," I chimed in quickly.

"Ruth," said my aunt solemnly, "there are a great many things I have never actually told you not to do, but which you know in your heart I shouldn't like, so don't make silly excuses. Now before we go any further I want you to promise me that you will never go out alone again at night as long as you live with me."

We both promised most earnestly.

"Very well, then," continued my aunt. "As long as you understand that, we will say no more about it. Now perhaps you are wondering how I came to know about it."

As a matter of fact, we thought we could guess, but we did not say so.

"Yesterday," said my aunt, "just after you had gone out, Terry's mother came to see me. She had a long story to tell me. She told me that some weeks ago she was in despair about earning some extra money to buy a blanket for her little boy, and when she saw those big rosy apples you took to Terry she decided to come at night and help herself. She did this once or twice, taking a few pounds from each tree so that your uncle wouldn't notice, and earned quite a little sum by selling them to the greengrocers in the villages round Tanglewoods. Then one night she met you in the orchard."

We looked guiltily at each other and wondered whether my aunt would be very cross with us for not telling. We weren't enjoying this secret much!

"You promised not to tell," went on my aunt, "which wasn't very sensible of you, because if you had told me all about it sooner I might have been able to help her sooner. But still, I know you meant it kindly. And then she told me that you went to see her and took her all your money. And you, Ruth, gave her your picture."

I blushed again. I was rather shy about my picture.

There was a long silence. The moon was rising behind the black pines, and the garden was full of little whispering breezes and rustles. But we sat quite still with upturned faces waiting for Aunt Margaret to go on.

"She came to see me and brought me the money because she said she felt as though Jesus the Shepherd in your picture was calling her, and she could get no rest until she answered him. And then we had a long talk and she told me all about that little boy of hers, who seems to be dying in that dark hovel of a home. I went to see him this morning and it's all true. She can't leave him to go to work, and she won't be parted from him to let him go back to hospital, and they are as near starving as one can be nowadays."

My aunt stared out into the twilight. She seemed to have almost forgotten us.

"And when she had gone last night, Philip and Ruth, I think the Shepherd spoke to me, too. I have not thought about him much for a long time, but last night he showed me a lot of things."

My eyes were fixed on my aunt's face, and I had drawn so close that she put her arm around me.

"He showed me a great many things I can't tell you about now, but I will tell you about two of them. He showed me a lot of money lying doing nothing in the bank, and he showed me an empty room all covered up with dust sheets, but with a beautiful window looking out over the plain with the sun shining in through it every morning, and the beech tree just outside."

I gave a little jump. "The best spare bedroom," I whispered.

My aunt nodded. "Yes," she agreed. "The best spare bedroom that's been empty for such a long time. But it's not going to be empty any longer, because we want to use it for the Good Shepherd. So the day after tomorrow, Terry and his mother are coming to live here with us for a time. Terry's mother is going to help me in the house, and Terry is going to lie by the window in the spare room and get some colour into his cheeks. It will be his very own room, and you and Philip shall help arrange it, and get it ready tomorrow. Would you like that?"

Should we like it? We were both so glad that we could not speak one word, but I think we must have looked very joyful, for Aunt Margaret laughed a little and seemed to understand. Philip's eyes, at any rate, were quite starry with happiness.

So we sat and talked until the moon swung clear of the pines and the last glimmer of light had faded in the west. Then Uncle Peter came and stood in the doorway and we flung ourselves upon him.

"Do you know?" we shouted joyfully. "Do you know?"

"Of course he knows," said my aunt, laughing. "You don't think I'd turn the house into a hospital without asking him?"

So we were hustled off to bed. We were told we needn't even wash, except for faces and hands, because it was so late – which was certainly a perfect end to a perfect day.

We spent most of the next day getting the room ready for Terry. We spring-cleaned it ourselves and made up the beds, one in the corner for Terry's mother and one by the window for Terry. We collected our nicest books and toys and arranged them where he could see them, and then hung up our brightest pictures on the walls. We picked the rosiest apples and the yellowiest pears and put them in a dish by his bed. Then we stood and looked round, and decided that it was quite perfect.

# 18

# Terry at home

Terry arrived in an ambulance, at teatime, and his mother came with him, carrying their few little belongings in an old tin box. My aunt had arranged for the ambulance, and Terry had been lifted and carried as gently as possible but, even so, he was tired out. And when they laid him in his bed by the open window and his dark eyes turned wistfully to the beech tree, his small face looked as white as the pillow on which he rested.

The rest of the summer holidays passed quietly. Terry seemed perfectly happy, and would lie for hours looking out of his window with his arms thrown around his head.

Philip was supposed to be working for a scholarship, so most of his evenings were spent at the dining room table with his school books spread out in front of him. At these times I would slip upstairs and sit with Terry. Sometimes I would put the light on and read aloud to him, but sometimes I would perch on the bed and, leaning my elbows on the sill, I would stare out into the dusk and talk.

We talked about a great many things, for Terry, now that he was too ill to do much else, thought a good deal. We often went back to those happy days in the wigwam, and talked about nests and animals. Sometimes we talked about the accident and about the hospital and the long, dreary days in the dark cottage. Sometimes we talked about my mother and father, and how pleased they would be to see Terry when they came home. Sometimes we just compared our thoughts – the odd thoughts that grown-ups probably forget about, and that only children tell each other.

"Ruth," said Terry suddenly, as we sat in the twilight one evening, "what's dying like?"

I shuffled my feet uneasily. "Oh, I don't know," I answered, "but I think it's very nice. At least, I think it's just like going to a beautiful place where Jesus is, and where everyone is happy. Why, Terry?"

"'Cos, I 'eard the doctor in the 'ospital say it," said Terry, looking round to see that no one else was going to come in at the door. "I told you once. He said, 'It's all up with 'im, poor little chap!' That means dyin'."

"But that was a long time ago," I objected.

He shrugged his thin shoulders.

"I ain't got no better," he replied. "Ruth, do everyone go there? Where you was talkin' about, I mean?"

"I'm not sure," I answered, slowly. "I think perhaps you have to ask the Shepherd, Jesus, to find you. I think you have to belong to him. But that is quite easy, Terry. You only have to ask to be found, like the sheep in the picture."

He frowned.

"I were a bad boy," he admitted, doubtfully. "I pinched ever such a lot of things whenever I could lay hands on 'em. The cops nearly got me once."

"I think it would be all right, all the same," I assured him. "But, Terry, I'll ask Mr Robinson to come and see you. He could tell you about it ever so much better than me."

There was a pause. Terry didn't seem particularly cheered by the prospect of Mr Robinson.

"Ruth," he said at last, "where's the picture – the one you gived us?"

"Oh, you mean my picture?" I answered. "I don't know, Terry. I suppose your mother's got it."

"I'd like ter look at it again," he said. "I told Mum to take it away 'cos it kind of fretted me to see that sheep stuck on the rocks and wondering whether maybe the shepherd couldn't reach it. But seein' as 'ow it's Jesus, I specs he could reach anywhere, couldn't he?"

"Oh, yes," I answered, with perfect confidence, "Jesus can reach anywhere. I don't believe anybody could stray away so far that Jesus couldn't bring them back. So you needn't worry about the sheep. It's quite all right."

"What I'd like," went on Terry rather dreamily, "would be a picture of that there sheep after the shepherd had took him up, when he was safe-like, in the shepherd's arms and being carried home. I'd like that fine."

"Would you, Terry?" I said eagerly. "I'll try to get you one. I'll look everywhere and see what I can find."

Terry gave a wan little smile and seemed too tired to talk any more. So we sat in silence until his mother came up to settle him for the night, and I slipped downstairs to see whether Philip had finished his lessons.

I did not forget my promise, and on the first Saturday of the autumn term I set out to ask Mr Robinson's advice about the picture. Philip had stayed at school to play in a football match, so I had to go alone.

Mrs Robinson was sitting at the window sewing, so I stopped and had a chat and a chocolate biscuit with her. The twins were rolling about in their playpen, and I couldn't leave without a game with them. So, by the time I eventually reached the church where Mr Robinson was arranging the table for the Sunday services, the afternoon was drawing on. I knew he usually had Saturday afternoons off, but I supposed setting out the communion table didn't count as work. Anyway, I felt that I must waste no time in unnecessary explanations.

"Mr Robinson," I started, walking up the aisle, very fast, "do you remember that picture you gave me?"

He stopped what he was doing and sat down on the steps. I sat down beside him. It was a rather nice thing about Mr Robinson. He always gave you his whole attention.

"Indeed I remember it very well," he replied. "Because, as you know, I have the same one hanging in my room."

"Oh, yes," I answered, "of course you have. But, Mr Robinson, I want to get the next picture to that one. Do you think it would be possible? Do you think there *is* such a picture?"

Mr Robinson looked very puzzled.

"I'm afraid I don't understand what you mean by the *next* picture," he said, gently. "Do you mean another picture by the same artist?"

"Oh, no," I answered. "I don't mind who's painted it. I mean a picture of what happens next, after the shepherd has picked up the sheep, and when it's safe in his arms. You see, Terry – our friend who got hurt and is living with us now – doesn't like my picture. It makes him feel unhappy because he says he can never feel sure when he looks at it that the shepherd will really be able to save that sheep. You see, the shepherd's arms don't look very long and the sheep is a long way down the precipice, and sometimes it bothers Terry. So I thought I'd try and get him the next picture, where the sheep is safe, and where there's nothing more to bother about."

Mr Robinson's eyes had never left my face while I was speaking and, when he answered, his voice was very earnest.

"I will try my very hardest to get Terry the next picture," he said. "But, Ruth, you mustn't let Terry worry about the sheep. Do you think you could teach him something from the Bible, if I taught it to you first?"

"Oh, yes," I answered, "I'm sure I could. I've taught him lots already. Is it about the Good Shepherd?"

"Not exactly," said Mr Robinson. "At least, it doesn't actually mention the Shepherd, but it's about him all the same. It's this: 'He is for ever able to save the people he leads to God.' Do you know what that means, Ruth?"

No, I didn't.

"Tell Terry that it means that however far the sheep had strayed, however high it had climbed, however low it had fallen, the Good Shepherd could still reach it. There are no people in the world, however naughty or however far away from God, whom the Lord Jesus cannot save as soon as they ask him."

I looked up quite satisfied. "I'll remember that and tell Terry, and then he needn't worry about that sheep any longer. Thank you, Mr Robinson."

"And on Monday," my friend promised, as we left the church, "I am going over to Hereford. I will see if I can find in the shops the picture you want."

I told Terry about what the clergyman had said, and Terry seemed glad. He promised to feel quite certain about the poor sheep getting safe home, because he knew now that even the worst precipices couldn't stop the shepherd finding that sheep.

But poor Terry was very tired that night, so tired that I stayed only a few minutes. His face looked even whiter than usual, and he kept screwing it up as though the pain was very bad. I knew his mother had hardly left him all day, and my aunt had been cooking wonderful little dishes to try to tempt his appetite, but it was all no good. Terry turned his face to the window and lay silent and uninterested.

Several days passed and the beech leaves outside began to fall rapidly. Terry seldom spoke, but he liked watching them whirling about and, although his mother sat beside him most of the time, he usually lay looking out. The doctor came two or three times during the week, but each time he looked so grave and sad that I dared not ask him how Terry was getting on, and when he would be able to play again.

It was one afternoon about teatime that I came bounding in from school to find that Philip was late. So, flinging down my satchel, I clattered upstairs and then stopped short at Terry's door and opened it softly, for during the past few days even I had come to realise that I ought to be quiet here.

But I stopped in amazement at the threshold, for beside the bed sat Mr Robinson, and Terry's drawn face was turned towards him with something like a smile on it, while he listened to a story about a tiger.

I drew up a stool and listened, too, until the tiger was dead and buried under a palm tree. Then Mr Robinson drew a flat parcel from under his coat. "We waited till you came to open this, Ruth," he said.

With eager hands I tore off the paper and string while Terry watched. When it was unwrapped and the picture lay before us in all its beauty we were so pleased that we did not say anything at all. We both just gave a little gasp and stared at it.

It was a framed picture of a meadow full of clean white sheep all walking one way and nibbling the grass as they went. In front of them walked a shepherd with a crook, and in his arms lay a little lamb peacefully asleep.

It was Terry who broke the silence.

"Where's 'e carryin' 'im to?" he asked suddenly, in his fretful voice.

"Home, Terry," answered Mr Robinson, with a look on his face that I did not then understand. "Safely through each day until they get home."

"Where's home?" went on Terry.

"It's the place where the Shepherd lives and where we see him face to face," Mr Robinson replied. "Shall I read you something about home, Terry?"

The boy nodded, and Mr Robinson took his New Testament out of his pocket and read in his slow, clear voice about a city where God lived.

"And he will wipe away all tears from their eyes, and there will be no more death, suffering, crying or pain."

There was another long silence, broken again by Terry.

"Coo!" he whispered thoughtfully. "No more pain! That won't 'alf be smashin'!" Then, after a minute's thought, he added,

"May everyone go, or only the good 'uns?"

"The gate is open for everyone who wishes to go in, and who belongs to the Good Shepherd," said Mr Robinson, "whether they've been good or bad. You see, the Good Shepherd died to make every one of us fit to go in. Do you remember the hymn? I'll say it, in case you've forgotten:

'He died that we might be forgiven,
he died to make us good,

that we might go at last to heaven,
saved by his precious blood.

There was no other good enough
to pay the price of sin;
he only could unlock the gate
of heaven, and let us in.'"

There was another silence, and then Terry whispered, "Tell me some more about them tigers."

And while he lay listening to the tiger story, Terry fell asleep with his hand on his picture, and Mr Robinson and I tiptoed out of the room.

Philip and I made a shopping expedition the following Saturday. We bought two daffodil bulbs for Terry, and some fibre to plant them in. We thought we would put them in a bowl on the windowsill so that he could watch the green shoots and the golden flower blossoms next spring. We sat on the floor burying them in the pots, and Terry lay watching us listlessly.

"Funny," said Philip suddenly. "You wouldn't think there was a daffodil hidden down inside this dead-looking old thing, would you?"

"No," I replied, "you wouldn't. There hardly seems room to pack it all inside. I'm going to bury mine near the top, and then it will come up quicker."

"It won't make any difference," said Philip. "It won't come until its proper time. And, when that comes, however far under the earth it's lying, it will shoot up at once."

I was about to argue this, when I caught sight of Terry's face. It was even whiter than usual and all twisted up with pain. I wriggled nearer the bed and took hold of his hand.

"Oh, poor Terry!" I cried. "Is it very, very bad? Shall I fetch your mother?"

He shook his head.

"No," he whispered. "She takes on so when the pain's real bad." Then with a little sob, he added. "Wish I could go to the place where there ain't no more pain."

"I think," said Philip softly, after an uneasy silence, "that we'll ask God to take away your pain, like in the Gospels when people came to him and he stopped their pains. Kneel down, Ruth, and let's try."

Philip had never prayed aloud before, and the words came very haltingly.

"Dear God, please take away Terry's pain. Please make him well soon. Amen."

Then we opened our eyes and looked hopefully at Terry, for we almost expected to see the shadow of pain pass at once. Terry's eyes were open already and fixed on his picture which now hung just above his bed.

There were many footsteps up and down in the house that night while we lay asleep, for my aunt and Terry's mother did not go to bed at all, and the doctor arrived just before midnight. But no one heard the feet of the Good Shepherd when he drew near and picked Terry up in his arms.

So Philip's prayer was answered in a way we had never dreamed of. For before the sun had risen again, while the stars were still high in the sky, Terry had left his twisted, suffering body, and all his pain behind him for ever. The Shepherd had carried him home.

# 19

# Mr Tandy explains

The path to the woods was almost overgrown with yellow bracken and completely arched by golden beeches. But I pressed on because I wanted to get right into the heart of it, far away from everybody, where I could sit and think about the strange things that had happened since Terry died.

I walked a long way, because I was not thinking where I was going. I just wandered, kicking at the damp leaves and brushing aside the yellow bracken and trying to forget that we had left Terry alone in the earth. But I could not forget. And when at last I came to a clearing where a great chestnut tree spread out its branches, I lay down on the roots and, resting my head against the trunk, I gave way to my sorrow, and my tears fell thick and fast on to the moss.

I was so tired and so miserable that I never heard slow, heavy steps rustling through the leaves, and I quite jumped when a well-known voice above me spoke to me.

"Why, little maid, little maid," said the voice, "what be all this about? Ye'll catch your death of cold a-lying there on the ground."

It was Mr Tandy. He stooped down and wrapped his big rough coat about me just as though I had been one of his own stray lambs. Then he sat down on the root, and I gave a very big sniff.

I had not seen Mr Tandy for a long while because he had left our district to go and work at the Cradley folds. I was very pleased, but very surprised, to see him.

Very glad to have someone to talk to after my lonely walk, I told the old man my whole story: all about Terry and his pain, and his picture, and how he had come to live with us and hadn't got better.

"I prayed so hard he would get better," I said despondently, "but it didn't do any good. God didn't listen, and Terry died."

"Little maid," replied Mr Tandy rather hesitatingly, "s'posin' you come to me and says, 'There's a little lame lamb down yonder what can't run about' – on account of the pasture being steep like, and the stones sharp. And s'posin' I comed down and picked up that there little lamb and carried him in my arms to another pasture where the grass was sweet and the ground easy-like, you wouldn't come and tell me as I hadn't listened to you, would you, now?"

I gazed at him dumbly; I was beginning to understand.

"Little maid," he went on, "the Shepherd took his lamb home, that's all. Ye've no cause to fret."

"But," I cried, my eyes once more filling with tears, "it didn't seem like that at all. I know you'll say Terry's in heaven but it didn't look like that to me. They buried Terry in the earth and we left him there, and it seemed so sad and lonely. How can Terry be with the Shepherd when we left him lying in the earth?"

The old man did not answer for a moment, and then he started scraping about with his hands in the leaf-fall as though he were looking for something. His search was rewarded and he held out a shiny brown conker in one hand, and an empty seed case in the other – a withered old thing with green prickles turning brown.

"Now tell me," he said, in his slow, thoughtful voice, "what's a-goin' to happen to the conker, and what's a-goin' to happen to the covering?"

"Oh," I answered, "the case will get buried in the leaves and then I suppose it will just wither away. It isn't needed any more. But the conker will grow roots and leaves and turn into a chestnut tree."

"That's right," said Mr Tandy, encouragingly. "Ye couldn't have said it better. Now, tell me this, little maid. When you see the young chestnut tree a-waving its little new leaves in the sunshine next spring, with the birds a-singing round it, and the rain a-watering of it, you ain't goin' to fret any more for that old case what's crumbled under the leaves, be you?"

"No-o," I answered, with my eyes fixed on his face. Once more I thought I understood.

"Well, then," said the old man, triumphantly, "you cease fretting for what you laid below ground – t'weren't nothing but the case. The laddie's a-growing strong in the sunshine up yonder, along of his Saviour."

His kind old eyes lit up with joy as he spoke. He threw down the conker and case, shouldered his axe and rose stiffly to his feet, because his knees were "full of rheumatics" as he had once told me. Then he unwrapped me and told me to go home.

"For if I don't get along," he said, "I shan't get that there gap mended up, and my sheep'll be strayin' out again. Goodbye, little maid, and God bless you."

I watched him as he moved off into the golden shadows of the wood, and then I stooped down and picked up the conker and its case. Clutching them tightly in my hand, I set off home rather fast, for I was cold and tired and the dusk was falling. When I reached our fields again the sky was aglow with orange light, and against the sunset stood a little black figure scanning the landscape. It was Philip, and he had come to look for me.

I ran to him and slipped my hand into his, and we walked along in comfortable silence. As we climbed the stile, he glanced at my other hand.

"What are you holding so tightly?" he asked curiously. I unlocked my fist and held out my new treasure.

"It's a conker and its case," I said shyly, "and it's like Terry. Mr Tandy told me so."

"Why's it like Terry?" asked Philip.

"Because," I answered, finding it difficult to explain, "what we put in the earth was like the case. It doesn't matter because Terry didn't need it any more. The inside part that's alive has gone with the Shepherd, so I'm not really sad about it now. Mr Tandy said it was like a lamb being taken to another field where the grass is nicer."

Philip nodded understandingly. "I see," he said, "and I'm glad you're not sad any more."

When we got home, we found that my aunt had lit a fire in the nursery, and she, Terry's mother, Philip and myself were going to have supper. It was a lovely, picnicky sort of supper with hard-boiled eggs and treacle, gingerbread, rosy apples and pears, and hot cocoa. I had been for a long walk and Philip had been playing football, so we were both starving. We wriggled nearer the blaze and rubbed our shoulders together to show how much we were enjoying it. Even Terry's mother smiled faintly.

It was when we had eaten all we possibly could that my aunt, holding out her hands to the blaze, said softly, "Terry's mother and I have been making plans."

"Have you?" we asked, much interested. "Will you tell us?"

"Yes," said my aunt, "because it's a plan that you can both help in. In fact, I shall need your help a great deal. You see, now that little Terry has gone, we want to do something in memory of him. Terry was weak and ill, and we couldn't help him get better. But there are other weak, ill children whom perhaps we could help to get better. And now that I have Terry's mother to help me in the house, and Ruth is getting so handy, I was thinking we'd try to find some of these children and have them here in the holidays. I used to know someone who worked in a prison in London, and I think he could help us. I thought I would write to him and ask him to find two or three children who needed good food and country air, and invite them here for Christmas. We would give them as lovely a time as possible. Would you like it, Philip and Ruth?"

We thought it a wonderful idea, and both began to talk at once, eagerly planning what we would do to make it a happy Christmas for them. It was a great relief, for somehow, since Terry died, we had almost felt as though we ought not to talk about other things. But now we could talk freely and happily about this, for it was all because of Terry and somehow part of Terry.

So we planned about Christmas stockings and Christmas carols and Christmas dinners and Christmas trees. We felt our cheeks getting redder and redder in the firelight and I'm sure our eyes grew brighter and brighter.

"Auntie," I cried at last, cuddling up against her, "it *is* a good idea. How *did* you think of it?"

"Well," replied my aunt, "you are fond of 'Shepherd' verses, so I'll tell you how I thought of it. It was the morning I went to visit Terry for the first time. As I walked through the woods I remembered a verse I had forgotten for years. It is what the Lord Jesus said to one of his disciples just before he went back to heaven. He said, 'Feed my lambs', and that's why I wanted Terry to come to us so badly. Then when he died, I said to myself, 'This lamb doesn't need me any more; but there are plenty of others…'"

She stopped and stared into the fire. I held my hands out to the blaze, and we all sat thinking our own thoughts – sad thoughts about Terry, but all mixed up with happy thoughts about Christmas and the future.

The phone rang and startled us all, and my aunt went out to answer it. She was gone for some time. When she returned she was laughing, and her face looked most mysterious.

"Another piece of news," she announced "and this is the very nicest piece of news we've had for years."

We both stared at her in astonishment. Then suddenly Philip jumped to his feet and made a dash at her.

"I know!" he shouted. "I can guess! Mummy and Daddy are coming home!"

Auntie nodded. "Yes," she answered "you've guessed right first time. They will be here in time for Christmas."

Philip's face, flushed with the firelight, was radiant with joy. But I stayed perfectly still with my hands clasped on my knees. I suddenly felt miserable and obstinate, and all my old fears came back to me. I remembered Aunt Margaret's words of long ago, how she had said that I should be such a disappointment to my mother. I didn't want to meet her. She would like Philip better and I should be cross and unhappy and jealous again. And things were just beginning to get comfortable. I turned my head away and looked gloomily at the coal scuttle.

Philip gave me an impatient little shake.

"Aren't you pleased?" he almost screamed. "Why don't you say so?"

I gave a little shrug of my shoulders.

"Yes, I'm pleased," I replied, because that was what everyone expected me to say. Then I got up, because I wanted to get away from them. "It's bedtime," I said, coldly. "Goodnight, Aunt Margaret."

But it wasn't really goodnight, for half an hour later Aunt Margaret came softly to where I lay in the dark, and knelt by my bed.

"Ruth," she whispered, and her voice sounded all troubled, "why aren't you glad like Philip?"

I wriggled uncomfortably, feeling shy. I buried my hot face in the pillow. But my aunt did not go away. She waited patiently and, seeing that she really expected an answer, I whispered back.

"You said she wouldn't like me, and I don't suppose she will."

"Oh, Ruth!" cried my aunt. "I never said that! I said she would be disappointed when you behaved rudely and selfishly, but that was a long time ago. I know you have been trying hard to be good, and something has certainly made a difference to you. I have felt much happier about you lately. And of course your mother will love you dearly."

I stopped wriggling and lay quite still. I had suddenly stopped feeling shy.

"I know what it is," I answered quietly. "It's my picture. It's knowing the Shepherd that's made the difference."

"Yes," agreed my aunt, "you're right. Your picture, and learning about the Shepherd, have made a tremendous difference to all of us."

# 20

# A perfect Christmas

It was Christmas evening. We had had such a happy day that I kept having to stop and tell myself that it was all really true.

Mother and Father had arrived just a fortnight before. Philip and I had missed school and gone to Liverpool with Uncle Peter to meet the boat. We had been on a moving staircase, and we had stayed in a hotel where we had chicken and coffee-ices for supper. We had gone up to bed in a lift and the lift man had let Philip work it. Then we had been wakened early, and gone down to the Merseyside in a wet, windy dawn. We had watched the passengers streaming down the gangway of the great liner, until Uncle Peter had suddenly said, in a quiet voice, "Here they come," and there were Mother and Father showing their passports at the barrier.

Philip, absolutely trustful and joyful, had flung himself straight into Father's arms, and had then turned to Mother and hugged the hat right off her head. But I stood still, because I wanted to be quite sure of everything first; and when Mother ran towards me I looked up into her face and suddenly knew that I had found something I'd been wanting all these years without knowing it. I was so overcome with this discovery that I just went on staring up at her, and she didn't hurry me. She waited, looking down at me, until I was ready and held up my arms to kiss her. Then she stooped and drew me to her. There on the quayside, with the rain falling, and the crowds jostling, and the foghorns wailing, she told me in a whisper how much she loved me. I made up my mind, then and there, that I was never going to be parted from her again.

Then, I had one hand in Mother's and one in Father's, and Philip pranced round us like an excited puppy. We made our way back to the hotel, had kippers and toast and marmalade for breakfast, and nearly missed the train home.

And now it was Christmas evening and the great moment of the day was approaching. We had opened our stockings, and been to church, and eaten turkey and Christmas pudding until we all felt full to bursting. We had been for a walk on the hills in the afternoon with Father and Uncle Peter, and had come back very hungry, as though the lovely dinner had all been a dream. We had had tea by soft candlelight, Father had cut the cake with his Indian dagger, and we had all pulled crackers. But little Minnie, one of the London children, didn't like the bangs. She had been carried out screaming, and fed with chocolate biscuits in the kitchen by Terry's mother. Now Auntie was saying, "Run away for five minutes, children," and Mother was saying, "Go into the kitchen and see how Minnie is getting on," and Father was saying, "Anyone who comes into the drawing room will be eaten by a big brown bear," and Philip was pinching us all in turns and saying, "Come on everybody, now's our chance."

So when the drawing room door was safely shut on the grown-ups, we slipped on our coats and tiptoed out of the front door. The world was quite silent and the starlight lay silver on the snow. Philip looked at us intently and hummed the note, and then we all threw back our heads and started singing.

> "The shepherds had an angel,
> The wise men had a star,
> But what have I, a little child,
> To guide me home from far,
> Where glad stars sing together
> And singing angels are?"

We sang the carol right through, and I kept on thinking that the baby Jesus was now *my* Shepherd. The Shepherd, who was going to look after me day and night, and carry me home some day to where Terry was. I looked out into the wide white world with its snow, and smiled. I knew that I was perfectly safe for ever and ever.

But the carol was over and another of the London children, Alfie, was hammering excitedly on the door. It was flung open, and there in the hall, under the mistletoe and holly, were Mother and Auntie in paper caps, and Father and Uncle pretending they didn't know it was us, and Terry's mother with tears in her eyes and little Minnie clasped tightly in her arms.

"Did you like it?" we shouted. "Did you really think it wasn't us?"

But at that moment a piercing shriek from Alfie's little sister, Lizzie, made everybody jump. She had caught sight of something through the open drawing room door and was making for it. With one mind we fled up the passage behind her and crowded in. The candles on the beautifully decked Christmas tree were alight and shedding a rosy glow over the dark room.

It was so pretty that we stopped shouting, and sat down quietly, cross-legged on the floor, while Father started giving out the presents.

Soon it was our turn. Father took a square parcel from the pile at the bottom of the tree, and handed it to Philip.

"Open it carefully, Phil!" he warned. "It's very fragile."

Philip annoyed me by taking a long time over the unwrapping, but he always liked to spin out his pleasures for as long as possible. However, at last it came to light, and Philip made a funny noise in his throat like something trying not to explode. It was a black Kodak camera, just like the one we had so often gazed at in the chemist's shop.

"Philip!" I squealed. "You've got it!" Then I stopped short, for of course it was my turn now. Father had selected a flat, hard parcel and was holding it out to me.

Everyone crowded round to watch as I, unlike Philip, tore the wrappings off as quickly as possible and gave a little gasp of delight.

It was my own picture, but not a crumpled, torn postcard one. It was a big, beautiful copy in a carved wooden frame for me to hang over my bed and keep for ever. In fact, it was just like the one in Mr Robinson's study.

The grown-ups opened their presents after that, and seemed as pleased as we were. They were mostly home-made things and we were very proud of them: fretwork bookends for Uncle Peter, a purse for Aunt Margaret, a blotter for Father and a hot-water bottle cover for Mother. Terry's mother was presented with a highly coloured embroidered hanky sachet, which she admired very much indeed.

Of course there were other presents, too, but these were the main ones.

Philip and I helped clear up, and then Philip and Father sat down on the sofa together and looked at Philip's bird book for about the tenth time. But it was different now, because the camera lay in Philip's lap and they were planning the photos.

I wandered off by myself with my picture in my arms, and climbed the stairs. I wanted to curl up behind the curtain on the landing windowsill and look at the Christmas stars and snow, and listen to the bells that were ringing from the church nearby. But when I reached my hiding place, I found that Mother had got there first, and that was even better than being alone. So I climbed on to her lap and held up my picture, because I wanted us to look at it together.

"Isn't it beautiful?" I asked.

"Yes," replied my mother, "but what made you love it so specially, Ruth? Tell me about it."

So I told her rather shyly, and she listened, looking out over the snow, until I had finished.

"And it's not only me," I ended up. "He found me first but after that he found Philip and Terry's mother, and he found Terry, too, and carried him right home. And, Mummy, he sort of found Aunt Margaret, too. At least, I think she had forgotten about him a bit, and when she saw the picture it reminded her of him again."

"Yes, I think it did," answered Mother, "and do you know, Ruth, I also want to learn so much more about him. Won't it be lovely, all learning together? Sometimes, far away in India, I used to kneel down and pray that somehow you would get to know about him. But I never felt I knew enough to teach you myself."

I looked up quickly.

"Did you really?" I exclaimed. "Then I suppose that's why it all happened. I suppose you sort of sent him to us. I'm glad it's like that, because it makes it even nicer than it was before."

I laid my head against her shoulder, and we sat quite quietly looking out. I think I nearly fell asleep, and in a half-dreaming way I saw us all sought and found, and following through the green meadows in Terry's picture: Mother and Father, Auntie and Uncle; Mr and Mrs Robinson and the twins, their tiny feet stumbling through the daisies; old Mr Tandy with his flock behind him; Terry's mother; Philip and me; Alfie and Lizzie and Minnie – because I had promised to tell them all about my picture in the morning; and, in front of us all, the Good Shepherd with the wounded hands leading us on to a Land far away, where Terry was, perfectly strong and happy.

# Treasures of the Snow

Annette knew that she could never forgive Lucien for what he did to Dani, and she was going to make sure that no one else forgave him either. But what is she going to do when she is lying injured in the snow, miles from home, and Lucien comes past? Will she accept his help?

ISBN 978 1 84427 298 3
Price £5.99

# The Mystery of Pheasant Cottage

Lucy has lived with her grandparents at Pheasant Cottage but she has dim memories of someone else. Who was it? What are her grandparents hiding from her? Lucy is makes her mind up to find the answers, but it turns out to be harder than she expected.

ISBN 978 1 84427 297 6
Price £4.99

These books are available from your local Christian bookshop, SU Mail Order (01908 856006) or at www.scriptureunion.org.uk/shop